1 9 9 3

OTHER BOOKS BY GEORGIA SAVAGE

The Tournament

Slate and Me and Blanche McBride

The House Tibet

THE

ESTUARY

GEORGIA

SAVAGE

GRAYWOLF

PRESS

First published 1987 by University of Queensland Press,
Box 42, St. Lucia, Queensland, Australia

Excerpts from this novel have appeared, in slightly different forms, in
Quadrant, the *Bulletin,* and *Tabloid Story.*

Publication of this volume is made possible in part by a grant provided by the
Minnesota State Arts Board through an appropriation by the Minnesota State
Legislature, and by a grant from the National Endowment for the Arts.
Additional support has been provided by the Jerome Foundation, the
Northwest Area Foundation, the Mellon Foundation, the Lila Wallace-
Reader's Digest Fund, and other generous contributions from foundations,
corporations, and individuals. Graywolf Press is a member agency of
United Arts, Saint Paul. To these organizations and individuals
who make our work possible, we offer heartfelt thanks.

Published by G R A Y W O L F   P R E S S
2402 University Avenue, Saint Paul, Minnesota 55114.
All rights reserved.
Printed in the United States of America.

I S B N   1-55597-172-5

9 8 7 6 5 4 3 2
First U.S. Printing, 1993

Library of Congress Cataloging-in-Publication Data
Savage, Georgia.
The estuary / Georgia Savage.
p.   cm.
I. Title.
PR9619.3.S274E7   1993
823—dc20   92-30147

For my son, Ron

TABLE OF CONTENTS

IRENE

1

I'd forgotten how cold Brisbane can be in August. As the hired car pulled up and we got out beneath a cloud-streaked sky, I shivered inside my coat. There were tombstones everywhere and the noise of a jet passing overhead bounced at us from the surrounding hills.

My brother and I went into the chapel. An attendant in a grey suit was standing just inside the door. He nodded at us but didn't speak. The pews were all empty so Bart and I went to the front one and sat. Before us was a stage and lying on it was Irene's coffin. It was decorated with a spiky wreath of red and orange flowers — the kind that she'd disliked. Behind the coffin was a velvet curtain.

Bart cleared his throat and I turned to look at him. In his dark suit and tasteful tie he looked very much the solicitor. At the same time his face showed the strain of a rushed trip from Rockhampton and two days spent arranging our mother's funeral.

Feeling my eyes on him, he turned to me and said, "She died in the garden, you know. She wouldn't have felt anything."

"What do you think caused it?"

"The hemorrhage? God knows." Soft music began to

play. "The doctor said she could have had a slow leak in the brain for months." Bart was about to say more but stopped because a clergyman was coming through a door beside the stage.

He walked over to us, introduced himself as Griffiths and talked a bit about the weather. Then he asked if we were expecting any other mourners. Bart explained that Irene wouldn't have wanted others.

"We'd better start then," said Griffiths and he went to stand in front of the stage. The music stopped. He faced us and made a short speech about Irene, calling her by her Christian name though they'd never met. I turned to look behind me. The attendant had disappeared.

Griffiths half-turned towards the stage, closed his eyes and began the twenty-third Psalm. At the end of it, the velvet curtain parted, loud music filled the chapel and slowly Irene's coffin moved away from us. With a little shock I recognised the music. It was the theme from *2001: A Space Odyssey*. A laugh shook me. I bit my mouth to keep it in and felt Bart's hand close on my arm. I looked at him again. His face was still and he was staring straight ahead. When I turned back to the stage the curtains were swishing shut.

Later in the car I asked Bart whose idea the lift-off music had been.

"Mine," he said. "I thought you'd like it."

"I did, but it made me laugh."

"Yes, I should have foreseen that."

"Did Mr Griffiths object?"

"Not at all. He said some people ask for Rod Stewart." Bart gave a grunt of laughter himself.

"I didn't feel anything in there," I told him. "About Irene. In a way it was as if I didn't know her."

Bart didn't answer and I went on, "I visited her a bit, you know, in later years. It never worked out though.

4

At first we'd be delighted to see each other but within two days the visit would fall apart mainly, I think, because when we'd exhausted the subject of my Clare and your two kids we had nothing to talk about. Then I'd sit downstairs consoling myself with a gin or two and she'd be upstairs watching telly in that eyeshade which made her look like a dealer in a backstreet gambling joint."

"You'd been apart too long and anyway, you always were oil and water."

"I suppose we were but never mind — you loved her, didn't you?"

"For a long time I did," he said and after that neither of us spoke until we reached the city.

Instead of going to the hotel where we were staying we went to the Regatta. I don't remember being there before and I've no doubt it was Bart's first visit since his student days. The place was nearly empty and we were able to get a table on the veranda. A grand-prix rush of traffic went past us every time the lights on the next corner changed but after being at the crematorium I think we were both relieved to be where we could see the river and some trees.

At first we didn't talk about Irene. We talked instead of our respective lives. Bart, who was working for a mining company in Rockhampton, said how much he liked being there. "I'd sell the house in Brisbane and stay for good," he said, "but I suppose the kids will want to come back here later on."

When he left me to get a second lot of drinks I watched his straight back as he went, and realised that apart from knowing he liked Test cricket and John le Carrè novels, I knew little of what went on inside my brother's head. That wasn't surprising — in the past eighteen years we'd met no more than twice and then only briefly. I guessed

5

though that he cared about what he called correct behaviour and because of that I was still astonished by his choice of funeral music. While I was trying to work out what lay behind it, memory whipped me back to the time when I was eight and Irene climbed onto the table in her workroom and sang for Bart and me. She sang a ditty called "My Nellie's Red Drawers". ("There's a hole in the middle/For her to do piddle/My Nellie's red drawers.")

If Irene had sprouted horns and a tail I couldn't have been more surprised. She was a beautiful woman who specialised in being remote and flowerlike. The table-top performance was so out of character I didn't know whether to be shocked or delighted. Mixed emotion made me scream with laughter. I laughed until I was red in the face and then Bart punched me to shut me up.

At the time Hal, our father, was in hospital because of an old war injury. He was the family clown and we were miserable without him. Whether Irene was trying to cheer us up or whether having the stage to herself went to her head I still don't know.

The next day when we visited the hospital I rushed ahead to blurt the story out to Hal. Irene, hurrying in behind me, denied it and Bart had the presence of mind to back her up. For the first time in my life Hal was disappointed in me. He couldn't understand why I'd made up such a crazy story. I knew I hadn't made it up and that was probably the moment when I began to lose my childhood innocence.

I suppose most little girls think their mother beautiful but there's no doubt that mine was. Old photographs I have prove it. She was slim and dark with heavily-lidded hazel eyes, an elegant nose and a mouth that was thin but pretty just the same. At the corner of her jaw there was a little cluster of beauty spots in the shape of the

Pleiades. Irene was proud of them and when photographed always tilted her head slightly so that they showed.

As for me, old snaps show that I was all eyes, hair and mouth. I don't think Irene liked me much. It may have been my imagination but sometimes when I came upon her unexpectedly in the house she seemed to go white. I blamed myself for that, not her. Bart was only seventeen months old when I was born. His birth was a difficult one and the last thing Irene wanted was another baby so soon. She loved Bart though and even as a child I could see why. He was tall like Hal but with her looks. To top it off he was a bright student and a whiz at sport.

The whiz in question put an end to my total recall job by coming back to the veranda with two more whiskies. It was obvious that he'd been thinking about Irene too because as he sat, he said, "She had a personality change after Dad's death, you know. Put on a new persona the way someone else puts on new shoes."

"I think that happens to a lot of women."

As if I hadn't spoken, Bart went on, "The pale linens and pearls disappeared. She cut her hair and began wearing those floral beach pyjama things."

"Fairly normal behaviour, surely, for someone living at the seaside."

"She wasn't living at the seaside then. She was still living in Brisbane." Bart pushed my drink across to me. "Those pyjamas and big straw hats caused quite a stir in this old town I can tell you."

"She'd probably always wanted to dress that way and Hal wouldn't let her."

"Perhaps, but what about the lies?"

"Lies?"

"The ones she told about herself when she got to The Estuary?"

7

"About Grandma being a concert pianist, and Irene as a baby travelling the world in an outsize picnic basket?" I began to laugh. "I rather liked that."

"You would." Bart picked up his glass and tossed down a mouthful of whisky.

"Come on, be fair," I said. "She'd obviously been dying to be somebody for years. After all she was an extremely creative woman who'd had very little attention in her life. With Hal gone, she went overboard, that's all."

"Yes, and promoted him to colonel. Did you know that?"

Laughing, I said, "I knew she made a little shrine to him on top of the television set. She had a few dried wood-roses there along with a photo of him in uniform and his medals mounted on velvet. The sort of thing Hal wouldn't have done in a pink fit."

"God knows why, but the military connection became a big thing in her life. She started having her cronies in each Anzac Day for sherries and 'The Last Post'." Bart allowed himself a grin at that piece of information. Still grinning he nodded in the direction of the river.

I turned and saw a rowing eight gliding past. Now and then the wind brought us snatches of the cox's chant and we sat without speaking until we could no longer hear it.

As I turned back to Bart, he said, "She never forgave me for getting married, you know."

"I guessed as much."

"You don't know the half of it." Holding my eyes, he lifted his glass and drank. "For months she made Felicity's life a misery."

"In what way?"

"She'd leap out of her chair and drench the room in insect spray because she knew Felicity had a violent allergy to it. That sort of thing. I think it was the way she treated Liss that made me stop caring for her."

There were ironies for me in that remark but I let it pass.

"Remember the wedding?" said Bart.

"No, dummy, I don't. I was languishing back in Maryston with Murray Valley fever."

"Of course. I'd forgotten. Well at first Irene refused to have anything to do with it. Pretended in fact that it wasn't happening but turned up on the day looking stunning in gold Persian trouser things made of silk. No one could take their eyes off her and after the ceremony she sat on the terrace at Hoad's telling anyone who'd listen that her family had owned tin mines in Bolivia and that she'd grown up in a household which boasted a chauffeur and a tutor as well."

"Surely no one believed her."

"Of course they didn't."

"Did Irene realise that?"

"Not a bit of it. When Felicity and I left she'd launched into some rubbish about the tutor stealing Grandma's rhubarb wine. She said, for God's sake, that he hid the bottles in the top of the piano."

I was laughing again. "It's funny though, isn't it?"

"That depends on your sense of humour." He paused and gave me a look I couldn't read. "I haven't told you the bad part yet."

Still amused I said, "I'll steel myself," and took a gulp of whisky.

Bart shifted a bit in his chair in a way which reminded me of Hal on the odd times when he'd had something weighty to say. "You remember, don't you, that when Grandma died, Irene got the hotel?"

I nodded.

"She sold it and with the proceeds bought the place at The Estuary. There was still money left over though and

9

by the time she got rid of the house here and moved she'd have had somewhere in the vicinity of seventy thousand. Right?"

"I don't know. I suppose so. I hadn't thought about it."

"Well she must have, and now except for eight thousand in bonds she couldn't cash, it's gone."

The announcement, underlined by the grim look on Bart's face, seemed to me funnier than anything I'd heard that morning. I laughed immoderately and went on laughing until some girls at a nearby table began to stare.

Through the laughter, I said, "I remember being on the tram with Irene once. I was about four and had on a blue dress with smocking on it and little pearl buttons. I was standing next to her and I looked carefully at the skin on her cheek and told her it was like a peach in Mr Gorrman's shop. Everyone around us laughed and I couldn't understand why." By the time I'd finished speaking, I wasn't laughing any more. I was crying.

His face impassive, Bart handed me the handkerchief from his breast pocket. I took it and moved my chair a quarter turn so that the watching girls could no longer see my face. Thinking *I still don't know myself at all*, I went on crying while a group of cars flew past, followed in a little while by a young man on a bicycle with a baby in a fur-lined cap strapped to his back.

I calmed down in the end and was putting the hankie away when Bart said, "Shall I tell you about the money?"

I nodded but didn't turn back to him.

"Irene put it into good stock — I know that because we talked about it at the time. Yesterday Giles, her bank manager, told me that about eighteen months ago she started converting it to cash and putting the bulk of it in her cheque account. He said that more than once he advised her against such a course and was quickly put in his place. Irene told him that she'd always managed her own affairs and could go on doing so without his help."

I moved my chair then so that I could see him. "And she spent the lot?"

"I doubt that she spent much of it. If she did, there's nothing to show for it. I think it more likely that, egged on by her mates, she made a series of foolish investments. Giles said that just before Christmas last year she took out thirty-five thousand in one hit. My guess is that she gave it to someone to make petrol from pig shit or something." He paused. "You realise that between us we're down a small fortune."

"I don't feel we deserved much, Bart. I know I didn't."

"That's not the point, though, is it?"

"I think it is."

He hit his fist softly on the table. "I should have kept a check on her — looked into her affairs now and then."

"But why would you? She appeared to manage well in the past."

"She wasn't managing too bloody well when she got rid of all that cash."

I studied his face, seeing there the likeness to Irene and over it, a tracing of Hal. More gently than I'd spoken before, I said, "You think, don't you, that what the doctor called a slow leak in the brain caused the change in her?"

"What other explanation is there?"

"That Hal was smarter than we knew. That he did a lot of the managing and let her take the credit."

While Bart was absorbing that piece of blasphemy, I leaned forward a little and said, "Look, as far as I'm concerned, she was *never* too damned rational."

11

Bart dropped his eyes. Then he spread his hands and spent some time looking at the palms. Finally he said, "She left the place at The Estuary to me."

"I thought she would. It makes sense — you're living in Queensland and everything." My voice was easy enough but I was surprised how sharply that last action of Irene's knifed into me. Pride made me keep the fact to myself and still speaking easily, I said, "What will you do? Sell it?"

The voice didn't fool Bart. He coloured, flicked his eyes to my face then away again. "It's not worth much and Felicity had some idea about your coming to live in it." He cleared his throat. "This morning on the phone she said that by rights half of it's yours anyway."

"Don't tell me the women's movement has reached Rockhampton." The joke flopped because the thought of my sister-in-law's loyalty made my voice shake slightly in mid-sentence.

Tersely Bart said, "For God's sake don't bawl again," and thinking that if I didn't pull myself together he might punch me for old time's sake, I took a deep breath and held it down.

"It's something to think about," said Bart. "Moving I mean."

When I didn't answer, he said, "You're not mad on your job. You told me that last night."

"It's true — I'm not."

"Up here you'd probably manage without one but you'd get something at The Estuary if you wanted it."

Again I didn't anwer and he said, "Is there some bloke down there?"

"Only Duffield."

Bart was waiting for me to go on so I said, "James Duffield. We've been lovers for a year or so."

"Is it serious?"

"Not really. I like him a lot, that's all. Funnily, he's a little like Hal. Same smile, same charm but he's married with two pretty rather popeyed daughters and for my part marriage was never on the agenda."

I think Bart was displeased at finding something in his sister's closet because his voice was terse again when he said, "And Clare, would she mind if you shifted?"

"I doubt it," I said and although I could see that he expected more, I didn't go on.

"So there's nothing much to keep you in Victoria."

"I suppose not, but one puts down roots, you know."

"You're young enough to haul them up." Bart was studying my face as I'd studied his earlier. (Did he find Hal and Irene on mine too?)

"Think about it," he said, "it's time you had a change."

"You may be right." I smiled at him. "Okay, I'll think about it."

He stood then in the way I guessed he did when he was ending an interview in his office. "Come on," he said "let's go into Indooroopilly and find somewhere decent for lunch."

I stood too and as we went along the veranda, I said, "It would be fitting if we found some little place where they served rhubarb wine from the top of the piano."

"And Anzac biscuits with the coffee."

Neither of us laughed. Then Bart took my arm and we went down the steps into the street.

2

As things turned out, I took Bart at his word and moved to Queensland at the end of the year. The sadness of leaving the Maryston Valley was softened by the fact that I loved Irene's old house at The Estuary. A white stuccoed place with a flat roof, it stood in a wildly sloping garden facing the Pacific. Its windows were double-decker Queensland ones which opened outwards from the bottom. When they were all sticking out, they looked like wings and the house seemed ready to fly.

Inside, the floors were stained a soft Chinese green and scattered with rugs I'd known since childhood. In hot weather, pairs of panelled glass doors allowed the living area to be made into one vast room.

Each day about noon a breeze came in from the ocean bringing with it smells of salt and seaweed and sometimes frangipanni. The venetian blinds began to chime then and kept it up until the breeze dropped again at night.

Downstairs there was an extra bedroom, a lumber-room and a laundry. In the lumber-room I found Irene's work-table. I don't suppose she'd used it for years but I could remember when it was the focal point of our house in Brisbane.

Irene was a dress designer who specialised in bridal

wear. Working long hours in the days when few married women had paid jobs, she more or less kept us. Hal, who had a small army pension, didn't work at all.

The table I found in the lumber-room used to stand bang in the middle of Irene's workroom. Scissors in hand, she'd walk around it eyeing a river of pearly satin which lay on it and fell from one end to form a lake on the floor. After several circuits she'd stand, one foot thrust forward, and concentrate on the material. Then she'd raise the scissors and move in. She always made the first cuts without the benefit of patterns or chalks or even a tape measure. I'm certain the idea of making a mistake didn't occur to her and because of that she almost never did.

As a child I loved the workroom and longed to run my hands over the bolts of silk and satin which stood in the cupboard under the window. I also wanted to touch the spools of sewing thread, each sitting on a peg of its own in a wooden rack. I didn't dare. No one in the house but Irene touched anything in that room. Occasionally Bart was called in to help her do what she called "finding the straight" on a length of material. I was never asked to help, but I had my own workroom in a corner under the house, where sunlight coming through the lattice made skinny diamond shapes on an old treadle sewing machine. The top of that machine was my cutting table and there I sliced into scraps of material while making Irene-remarks, such as "On the bias from the hip", to my doll who sat watching.

I played there off and on until the Sunday Irene found her spools of thread thrown in a corner of the workroom with the wooden rack on top of them. I saw the mess of cream and pink and gold they made when I was hauled upstairs to be charged with doing it. To me the sight was so awful that while accusations flew around my head like lightning, I kept quiet. Some child-intuition told me that what had happened was part of the dark adult world to which things like my mother's migraines and the kidskin apron in my father's Masonic bag belonged. When sentenced to a month without mango ice-cream and trips to the cinema, I accepted it as a judgment on my inability to please Irene in any way at all. And I went outside still without defending myself.

If the person who *did* throw the spools on the floor ever owned up, I wasn't told. But touching the smooth old surface of Irene's table almost thirty years later it seemed obvious to me that a fit of unbearable frustration had caused one of my parents to do it. Whatever the case, my punishment tailed off during the first week and had ended by the second. The memory of that day stayed with me though and I didn't ever go back downstairs to design clothes in the half-dark. Instead I played other games in the garden where the light was filtered through trees, not lattice.

The clothes Irene made were prized for their line and simplicity; the ones she wore herself were so perfect that at the age of nine I opted out of the race and started dressing as a boy. Hal was delighted at my sex-change and egged me on by taking me to his barber and having my hair cropped. Needless to say the wearing of khaki shirts and shorts was only bravado on my part. Whenever I was alone in the house I rushed to put on Irene's clothes and then posed and preened in front of the mirror.

Hal and Irene didn't sleep in the same room. My friends used to ask me about it with sly looks on their faces. I didn't understand why they were so interested and greeted the questions with a vacuity which must have astounded them. Apparently Hal was banned from the bedroom after my birth and if he visited Irene there

16

it was in furtive dashes at night when Bart and I were asleep. One thing was certain, Hal hadn't lost interest in women. He was mad about them. I think he was a flirt rather than a lover, but even my eyes which missed so much took in the fact that there was always some woman on the fringe of the family who was his buddy rather than Irene's.

About the time I started dressing as a boy, Hal's sister asked Irene to go into business with her. She wanted to open a shop in a swanky part of Sydney and make and sell clothes for small women. Irene, scenting a fortune, put our house on the market, but when Hal found out he flew into a temper and threatened to kill himself if she went ahead with the plan. Then he went away into the bush and hid at the place where he kept a few hives of bees. Bart and I were left at home in a state of terror while Irene searched the country roads in a taxi. At the end of the day Hal and Irene came home together. They were in unaccountably high spirits and the dress shop was never mentioned again.

In those days I was always pestering Hal to let me learn tap-dancing. As an art it wasn't socially acceptable in our circle and he held out against me for a long time. One afternoon when we were walking the dog in the park we met the local dancing teacher, Ettie Hayden. Ettie was tall and lithe with marvellous legs. A bit of her coat hem was hanging down and as I introduced her to Hal I prayed he wouldn't notice. It was the kind of thing that put him off someone for life. Ettie shifted her chewing gum and gave Hal a smile. It was a stunner. Hal goggled at her, made a few feeble remarks about the weather then whistled his dog and got it to do some tricks. I was so ashamed of him I wanted to die, but I forgot it the next day when he took me to Ettie's studio and signed me up for a year's lessons. Part of the bargain, of course, was that Irene wasn't to be told.

Altogether I had tap-dancing lessons for two years. Ettie took a shine to me — I think my clothes amused her. Sometimes after the other kids had gone she let me stay and dance with her. The buzz I got from dancing with Ettie in the big bare studio with chairs stacked in the corners was something I never got over. It makes me grin even now to think of it.

Somewhere in the second year of my lessons Ettie and Hal started an affair. I doubt that it progressed much beyond whiskies in the local and a few feel-ups. Ettie had a nineteen-year-old lover in the navy. He was a good ten years younger than she and had long dark eyes and a squashed Greek nose. Ettie was nuts about him and I guess she egged Hal on mainly for laughs. Whatever the case she was indiscreet enough to call at our house one day wearing a new fox coat and strappy shoes. Irene answered the door and that was the end of the dancing lessons. The end of me too for that matter. At the start of the next term I was sent to boarding school and for several years I spent my holidays at my grandmother's.

Grandma had a hotel at a place called Ely in the mountains. Ely was not much more than the pub, the butter factory and a few houses. It was a wet green place with shadows that closed in on it soon after lunch. Dozens of little trails led away into the forest and every half mile or so there was a fast-running creek.

In her heyday I think Grandma was even better looking than Irene. The things I remember of her are smooth olive skin and sombre eyes which occasionally lit up and knocked the breath out of you. She had only a yardman and a kitchen-maid to help her run the hotel, so she often worked an eighteen hour day. In the afternoons she worked in the garden; she said pottering there saved her sanity. She trained fruit trees to stand like Picasso figures against the back wall of the pub and she looked after a hive of bees Hal had given her. Every so often she put on leather gloves and a beekeeper's hat and after quietening the bees with a gadget which belched smoke, she took frames of wax-capped honey from the hive. In the kitchen she'd uncap the honey with a hot knife and let me have a mouthful of honey and wax. She was gentle, patient and kind. I should have been happy with her but I was not. I waited all the time for Irene to swoop down on us in a taxi and take me home. I imagined we'd arrive in high spirits the way she and Hal had done after his suicide threat. I thought she'd make up for my banishment by making me wonderful clothes and buying me sarsaparilla spiders. Of course none of it happened and I stayed at Grandma's.

To console myself, I used the upstairs veranda of the pub as a stage and spent a lot of time up there dancing. Nobody bothered me, least of all my grandmother. Occasionally, a drunk leaving the hotel in daylight would see me and send up some applause. Then, humiliated, I'd leap through the nearest window and hide until he'd gone.

Practically the only books Grandma had were the Scarlet Pimpernel ones. I read them over and over and when I wasn't dancing on the veranda I was rescuing French aristocrats from the guillotine. I did most of my rescuing at night when Grandma was busy in the bar. Her deaf white cat, Albert, usually played the part of the Dauphin.

One night as I stepped from the fire-escape with Albert buttoned inside my duffel coat, a hand grabbed the back of my collar. I was dragged a few steps then spun around to face the street light. Albert leapt out of my coat and rushed back to the hotel. I wasn't frightened, merely furious that someone had taken such a liberty with me.

I glared at the man who'd grabbed me but before I could speak, he said, "Ah, it's the androgynous child who dances on the balcony." His voice fitted so perfectly into my Scarlet Pimpernel adventure that my anger died and I stood gaping at him. It was Max Tischler, the Austrian sculptor who lived in the next valley. I'd seen him now and then in the hotel buying bottles of wine. His European clothes and haunted white face fascinated me but when I asked Grandma about him she fobbed me off by saying, "Don't worry about him. He's not a person for little girls to be interested in." After that, I was even more fascinated. In time, by asking discreet questions in the kitchen, I learned a lot about him. He'd come to Ely after being involved in some sort of trouble in the city. No one knew exactly what the trouble was and at first the locals accepted him with the silent watchfulness they kept for all strangers. But Max Tischler had the kind of stunning good looks gangsters have in French movies so it wasn't long before the Ely CWA ladies invited him to talk to them about art.

Max turned up for the talk with a pottery uterus under his arm. Inside it was a clay fetus surrounded by briny fluid. During the talk Max told the ladies that for the past eighteen months he'd sculpted nothing but uteri. Then he handed the one he'd brought with him to the nearest member of the audience and asked her to examine it and pass it along the row. Marie, Grandma's kitchen-maid, told me the uterus went along the row as if it were red hot, but when it reached the wife of the Methodist minister, she baulked and drew back her hands. The sculpture fell on the floor and smashed.

Coolly, Max stepped forward. He picked up the fetus and bowing slightly handed it to the woman. "Congratulations," he said "you've just given birth."

That night the CWA meeting was closed without supper being served and from then on Max was pretty much ostracised in Ely.

Marie told me that he went away a lot and seemed to have dozens of visitors from the city. When I insisted on details, all she could tell me was that the visitors were a weird mixture, from fat rich men in big cars to European peasants who tried to buy horseflesh at the local butcher's shop. She did tell me though that Max often worked for two or three days without stopping to sleep, and she hinted that he couldn't have done it without the help of some drug. In those days I knew very little about drugtaking and what I did know was somehow confused with thoughts of lovers exhausting each other with kisses in twilit rooms and things like the scent of Jamaican lilies. To find myself face to face with someone who'd tasted such delights was too much for me. The look on my face must have amused him because he laughed, then he said, "What were you doing on the fire-escape? Running away? Why don't you run to my place? I'll hide you." He was only a small man but his voice was rich and full — what Irene called a stagy voice. It broke the spell for me. "Don't be stupid," I said, and like Albert shot towards the hotel.

The next morning I looked up "androgynous" in the dictionary. I couldn't find it and asked my grandmother what it meant. She frowned and said, "I don't know." She was making pastry and looked up from her floury hands to ask, "Where did you hear it?"

But by then I was on my way outside. "At school, I think," I shouted over my shoulder.

From then on I began to spy on the valley where Max Tischler lived. I went there every day. I didn't go by road; instead I cut across the spicy bush behind the hotel and climbed the hill which separated our valley from his.

21

At first I merely hung around the trees at the top of the hill but gradually I began to work my way down the slope. Halfway down I found a flat place where I could lie and watch Max's cottage. It was half hidden by a ragged cloud of almond trees but I had a clear view of the barn he used as a studio. Sometimes I saw Max moving between the buildings and sometimes I saw him washing clothes in a dish on the back veranda then throwing them over a fence to dry.

He caught me as I suppose I'd meant him to. He came up behind me as I examined some carving on a rock I'd picked up. It was of two fetuses curled around each other like Yin and Yang.

"Do you like it?" he said, and I, copying the CWA ladies, dropped the rock as if it had burnt me.

He laughed, not a theatrical laugh but one of real amusement. Then he bent down and picked up the rock and looked at it himself.

"I've been watching you," he said, "getting a little closer every day. It was like watching a deer come for an apple." He looked up quickly and studied my face.

I went red and could think of nothing to say.

"You haven't told me if you like the carving."

I nodded.

"Then keep it. I did it for you."

"I wouldn't be allowed to," I blurted the words and he put his head back and laughed a laugh which was big and stagy but full of amusement as well. "Come along," he said, and he turned away from me and began to walk downhill. "I'll show you some more."

The inside of Max's cottage was a mess. I think he'd started to rebuild and redecorate all at once then given the lot up as a bad job. It was a shock to me to learn that anyone could live in such a way. Our house, Irene's house, always looked like something from the pages of

22

Elegant Living, and God help anyone human enough to leave the newspaper on the sitting-room floor. At Max's the wall between the two main rooms had been partly demolished. Plaster dust and bricks lay in a pile on the floor. He'd started to paint one of the other walls but stopped halfway. At the back of the sink he'd begun to put old-fashioned tiles; that job too had been abandoned. There were two tables, one covered with plates and dishes, the other with art materials and a dozen or so fetuses. The only orderly thing in the room was the mantelpiece which had nothing on it but two candlesticks and a painting of someone shot full of arrows. It was impossible to tell if it was a man or a woman and, in spite of the arrows, it was grinning like a lunatic.

"Did you do that?" I asked. Max was rushing around straightening papers and shoving fetuses into a carton. Without looking up he asked what I meant.

"The painting. The one over the fireplace."

"No."

"Who did?"

Instead of answering my question, Max threw the carton under the sink then rubbed his hands briskly. "What do you want to do?" he asked. "Stay here or go over to the studio?"

"I don't mind."

"Then we'll stay here by the fire and I'll do some drawings of you."

I nearly fainted with pleasure.

"Yes, that's it," said Max. "I'll dress you up and draw you." He shot through the gap in the wall and was back in a moment with a soldier's tunic. "Go into the bedroom and put this on."

I took the tunic and looked at it. "It's too big."

"I know. It'll look wonderful. Wait, I'll get you some shoes," and he dived at a carton in the corner and began to pull things out of it — a bent peacock feather, a striped jumper, a postcard so old it was yellow, then a pair of high-heeled silver sandals.

As I took the sandals, I said, "I'll look crazy."

"No, you won't. You'll look divine. Go into the bedroom. I promise not to peek."

For some reason the word "peek" worried me. It wasn't a word my family used. In fact I don't think I'd ever heard anyone use it. For a moment a doubt about what I was doing went through my mind, but it passed and I took the things and went through the gap into Max's bedroom. To my surprise it was neat and quietly furnished. The bed and wardrobe were made of solid dark wood and the material used for the curtains and bedcover was the kind of soft floral my grandmother liked. On the wall above the bed was a row of drawings of children. They were framed in gold and mounted on pale green watered taffeta. The room was so charming I forgot my dislike of the word "peek" and forgot too about the lunatic grinning from the kitchen mantelpiece.

"Hurry up," called Max from the other room, "put the jacket on and the shoes as well."

I stood in front of a cheval mirror and got into the tunic. It was certainly too big. The sleeves hid my hands and the hem came halfway down my thighs, covering my own clothes.

"I look crazy," I shouted, "I knew I would."

Max came through the hole in the wall. "No you don't," he said, "you look the way I want you to," and he knelt and helped me into the sandals.

I looked at myself again and repeated, "I look crazy."

"No," said Max, "you look beautiful."

"That's not true."

"You have something more than beauty, Vinnie — something else. Later, a lot of men will see it but they

24

won't know what it is." I was listening to his voice rather than his words. It was soft and throaty, not his big stage voice at all. Noticing the way I was watching him, he gave a shout of laughter, sprang to his feet, grabbed my arm and said, "Come on. Out of the bedroom. I want you to stand by the fire so the buttons on the jacket shine." And he took me back to the fireplace and posed me there.

"While I work, I'll give you something to listen to." Max wound up a gramophone so old it had a fancy tin trumpet on it. "Melba singing the Butterfly aria."

I hadn't heard Melba's voice but the one on the record was so thin and cracked I didn't believe it was hers. I was about to tell Max so when he said, "Don't move. I'm drawing you."

"I feel a fool."

"It doesn't matter."

"I don't know where to put my hands."

"I can't see them." Max gave another shout of laughter.

He did several drawings of me then let me look at them. I was disappointed. I'd expected to look like a fashion model, instead I saw a shadowed sexless creature wearing bomb-shelter clothes.

Max wasn't offended when I said so. He merely shook his head and said, "You've got a lot to learn, Vinnie, but if you like I'll do a pretty one of you to take home and hide."

He found me an old wine glass to hold. It was rose pink and had a chip in it. After he'd given it to me, he stood beside me and made a noise in his throat — a kind of European chirrup. Later I was to realise there was a sexual implication in the sound but at the time I took no notice. I was too busy staring at the frantic face of my grandmother looking through the window.

*   *   *

So I went home with Irene after all. We didn't go in a taxi, we went in the car with Hal. No one spoke. Once Hal tried to sing. He started "Danny Boy", but when he came to the bit, "From glen to glen and down the mountain-side", his song died of embarrassment. Irene sat with her feet together and eyes looking straight ahead. As for me, I watched the country go by with eyes that were hot and gritty from tears I'd been unable to cry.

Grandma had marched me barefoot back to the hotel and telephoned my mother. She arrived with Hal three hours later. She was dressed in an elegant black suit and had a little cravat of white at her throat. It looked like a judge's outfit. The first thing she did when she saw me was rush across Grandma's sitting-room and stab her foot into my shin. "You slut," she said. Then more slowly, "You slut."

I was horrified. To me a slut was someone like Patsy Larner who lived out on the road to the tip with a troop of fatherless children she couldn't be bothered feeding let alone keeping clean. I didn't answer Irene then or later. All the time she was packing my clothes and railing at me, I watched with eyes that were hot and dry, and didn't say a word.

Irene threatened to go to the police about Max but I knew she wouldn't. Hal, like me, said nothing; in fact he pretended the row wasn't happening and went outside to look at Grandma's bees. When we were leaving, Grandma tried to hug me but I pulled away from her. I thought she'd betrayed me and I felt that way for years.

At home, when Irene asked me over and over why I went to Max Tischler's house, I had no way of telling her. How could I when I didn't know myself? So I said nothing and inevitably that silence of mine damned me forever in my mother's eyes.

The upshot of my artist's-model episode was that I stayed at home with Hal and Irene. They didn't send me back to boarding school. Instead, I went to day classes like the rest of my friends. For some reason Irene started being nice to me. No, that's not quite right, she was both benevolent and condescending towards me as if she felt she'd won some major victory. But being called a slut by her had left a mark on me which didn't go away, and in four years time when I was old enough to go to dances I quickly became the wildest girl in my set as if determined to earn the title my mother had given me.

3

Sleepless on a night of thirty-five degree heat, I got up and went naked through the moonlit house to get some iced water from the kitchen. On the way back I met a pale version of myself in Irene's dressing-table mirror. What I saw was both like and unlike me — my body with its longish limbs and bat-shape of pubic hair. Above it, a face startlingly like my grandmother's. I went closer, bundled back my hair and examined my reflection. In the shadowy glass my eyes appeared to be brown though in fact they were what Hal had once called dark delphinium blue. It was my eyes, he said, that'd made him choose me from the band of children at the gypsy camp on Mount Tamborine. (As a child that was my favourite fairy story.) There in Irene's bedroom I could see that those eyes were the same shape as my grandmother's. So were my cheekbones, my nose and short upper lip. My mouth was fuller, longer, but my neck and the slope of my shoulders were identical with the ones I'd seen in her wedding photograph.

Delighted by the discovery, I stepped back and looked at the rest of myself, taking note of well-placed breasts, curved waist and white-scarred knee. (The knee lost most of its surface on my ninth birthday when Bart kidded me into curling up inside an old car tyre so that he could roll me down one of Brisbane's steepest hills.)

I leaned towards the mirror and after examining my face again acknowledged — for the first time — that my lifelong indifference to the cult of Irene's beauty had been possible only because I was secure in my own good looks, knowing instinctively that they were warmer, more flesh and blood as it were than hers.

I left the mirror then, went to the bed and sat on the side of it to ask myself how much the shape of one's face determines the shape of one's life. The question took me, inevitably I suppose, back to the day that I met Brook.

I was almost eighteen and wore my dark hair in much the same shoulder length bob as I do now. That day as far as my parents knew I was labouring over one of the matriculation papers in a hall at the old barracks. Instead I was sitting in the park as free as any bird in the tree above me. Brook, tall with classic good looks and a sweep of auburn hair on his forehead, came across the grass to sit on the other end of the seat. He had with him a book of poetry and a bag of fruit. Opening the book, he began to read and went on doing so until a young man without legs trundled past on a little wooden cart. When he'd gone, Brook and I exchanged a brief and agonised look and in a little while he asked me if I liked poetry.

I told him that I did but not enough to sit in a stuffy hall and answer questions about it.

He nodded in the direction of the barracks. "Are you supposed to be over there?"

When I said yes, he offered me a piece of fruit.

We talked for the rest of the afternoon and I learned that he was an engineer who didn't have a high opinion of the work ethic but had managed to get together enough money for a berth on a freighter leaving in a week for Copenhagen. From there he intended walking across country until he reached a Lapp village where he could live for a while and absorb the local culture. God knows what *I* talked about — nonsense I suppose, but anyway I made him laugh a lot and all the time I was careful not to look at him because I'd already fallen in love and was certain the fact was emblazoned on my face.

That night I took Brook home to dinner and Hal, who liked him immediately, helped me make up a story for Irene about how we'd met. She swallowed it and believing Brook would soon be Europe bound was surprisingly gracious to him. But instead of leaving on the freighter, Brook stayed in my home town and the day before the exam results came out, he and I caught a plane to Hobart and there at the end of the world we were married. I might add that I was pregnant although I wasn't certain of it at the time.

Because I was under age the marriage was invalid and Brook and I had to trek back home to face Hal's disappointment and the fury of my mother. Finally they agreed to sign the necessary paper and we were married again.

The second wedding was at the registry office and the man who officiated turned out to be a cricketing friend of Brook's. Each time they caught the other's eye, they laughed and when that happened, Irene's face froze beneath the ribbons on her French hat. Years later in the house at The Estuary I still had no wish to look at that day in detail.

For a few weeks we lived with my parents — an arrangement which gave Brook and Irene a chance to scrutinise each other. Neither liked what they saw. What lay behind their dislike I don't know, probably nothing more serious than the imagined threat to a way of life.

30

Whatever the reason it soon took them to the level of childishness, and Brook, who was proud of never letting his cool slip, was as childish as Irene. At some stage she'd been foolish enough to draw Brook's attention to the beauty spots on her neck. "Like the Pleiades in Taurus," she told him. From then on he referred to her as Madam Starlight. Brook in turn was indiscreet enough to tell Irene that he'd come from an orphanage. It was the piece of ammunition she'd been waiting for and she had a lot of fun with it. Altogether it was a relief to the lot of us when Brook took a job in the mountains and we left.

In the tiny settlement at the foot of Mount Evelyn, I thought I was finally living life but in reality I was merely honeymooning. Occasionally even now I mourn the feeling of freedom I had — days spent walking mountain trails in search of wildflowers and things like eagle feathers, nights spent making love before a fire while music played on shortwave radio and sometimes snow fell outside.

No doubt in time such an existence would have palled but it didn't get the chance. When I was five months pregnant I was taken to the local bush nursing hospital with toxemia and there, in a moment of delirium, I called my mother's name. The next day some fool told Brook and as soon as I was well enough to travel he bundled me up and took me to the Maryston Valley in Victoria where we settled. I didn't see my family again for years, not that I cared. At that stage I didn't want anyone but Brook. I didn't even want the child I'd conceived but I had the brains not to say as much to Brook.

At his insistence I went to a series of prenatal classes at the Maryston Hospital. They were conducted by a nursing sister of less than five feet, who stood with her weight on her toes and spoke from deep in her throat.

31

She began by telling the class that Asian women the size of twelve-year-olds enter the hospital, squat, give a couple of grunts and bingo, produce their baby without any further fuss. While waiting for the implications of that lot to sink in, she let her eyes travel slowly along the rows of swollen summer faces watching her.

"The quicker the birth," she said, "the easier it is for the child because while it's happening the baby works as hard as you do." Putting her cupped hands together, she made a series of shapes with them too quick and complicated for us to follow. "That's the way its head changes shape as it comes down the birth canal." She ran her eyes over us again. "Any questions?"

No one responded. In my case I was too featherheaded to relate the things she said to my own body and I must admit that in that class and the ones that followed my thoughts were often somewhere else.

The child was due early in May but my labour began on the evening of April the twenty-fifth when I went for a pee and felt a small Niagara pouring out of me. When it stopped, contractions started. Finding Brook, I told him I thought the baby was about to enter the earth's atmosphere. He stared at me to see if I meant it, then panicked a little, putting me alone in the back of the car like the Queen Mother and the dog and my suitcase in front. On the way out of the drive he clipped the gatepost, making us laugh wildly.

The labour lasted twenty hours. Today, only filmclip flashes of that night and the next day remain with me. I remember a time of misery in a small blue room where nurses did what seemed a lot of unnecessary things to me. Later, rolling with pain, I was in another room and a sister with an angry face kept telling me not to be a spoilt child. A period of blackness, then another sister bent over me to say, "Where's your breathing, Mrs Beaumont? Where's your *breathing*?"

I remember too a time of vomiting and being given a glass of what tasted like full-strength raspberry cordial. I saw Brook at one stage. He was wearing a hospital gown with blood on it. (The next day he told me that the drip they'd put in my arm kept falling out and the blood on him came from the place where it had been.)

At two thirty the next afternoon my doctor called in an obstetrician. I didn't see him arrive but suddenly, capped and gowned, he was standing by my stirrup-hoisted legs. "Hang in there," he told me, "it won't be long. I think the shoulder's catching, that's all." Then he put what felt like his entire arm inside me and moved the baby. A few minutes later Clare was born — a wizened little version of Brook, blowing bubbles through the gunk in her mouth. When I saw her I turned my head away and wept for both of us.

I slept and woke some time in the night to find myself in a ward with another bed in it and another sleeping woman. The hospital was in half-darkness and the only sound was a thin hiccupping cry from the nursery next door. I recognised it as coming from my child in the way, I suppose, a cow in a herd recognises the bellow of its calf. For a time I tried to ignore it but in the end I got out of bed and on shaky legs went to the nursery. More brightly lit than the corridor, it had thirty cribs in it, many of them occupied. I went to the crying baby and not bothering to read the label on its crib, picked it up. When it felt my familiar flesh, the hiccupping cry stopped. In the quiet room with its rows of cocooned babies, Clare and I looked at each other and although common-sense told me that she couldn't see me, her unblinking Time-Lord eyes seemed to be studying me — summing me up. With an eerie little prickling at the back of my neck, I was certain that we'd known each other some-where before. The next moment I told myself the feeling came from too much pethidine but instead of returning Clare to her crib, I took her back to the ward with me and holding her in the crook of my arm went to sleep again.

Instead of blasting me when they found I'd kidnapped my daughter, the nursing staff greeted the escapade with a kind of boarding-school jollity. From then on they brought her to me whenever I asked and in next to no time I was nuts about her.

I don't remember Brook taking much notice of Clare when she was little. No doubt that's a case of selective memory at work, but perhaps not because by then he had Hannibal Ballinger in his life.

Hannibal, who was five when Clare was born, had wandered in our gate one Saturday and stood behind Brook in the drive while he rotated the tyres on his car. In those days she was fat and hardly ever spoke. The day they met, she didn't speak at all, just watched him as he worked and when he'd reached the last tyre and was ready for the wheelbrace, she handed it to him. In doing so she charmed him into a friendship which would satisfy the lonely child in her and the untapped teacher in Brook.

Hannibal lived with her mother and brother half a mile from our place. After the tyre-changing episode she must have watched for Brook's car because soon after he got home each day she'd turn up at our back door and follow him up and down the rows as he mowed or sit with him by the channel to watch the ibis feeding in the grass at the edge of the orchard.

So in many ways we had two children instead of the one we'd counted on and somehow from then on it was as if my cosmic clock had been tinkered with because the years began to fly. Looking back it seemed to me that it was always summer. In reality there were miserable winters to get through as well as short-of-money Christmases. There were times too, many of them, when Brook and I fought over things which didn't matter. Nevertheless, remembering it all that night at Irene's place I felt certain that if I could ask him he'd agree with me that the sun was always shining and the blossom in the orchard rich with nectar.

While living at The Estuary I could have spent a lot of time thinking about that period of my life, could have dwelt on Clare's obsession with ballet and the effect Pandora Hunt had on our lives. But there seemed no point in doing that and anyway as I said before, the years flew. Clare was four, then five and suddenly nine. My father Hal died that year and with the crassness of youth I told myself he'd been lucky to die bang in the middle of life as he did. (His heart stopped at the races where he'd gone with someone else's wife.) Before long fate was to teach me a bitter lesson about such a way of thinking because two years later Brook died and when that happened I wanted to die too.

In the days that followed I thought of killing myself, even worked out how to do it. But I didn't because I knew Brook would expect me to go on. I always had him fooled into believing that I had a lot of guts and it seemed to me the time had come to act as if it were true. Besides, I'd worked out that if there was one chance in two hundred million of us meeting again, even in the form of jellyfish, I didn't want to blow it by behaving like a coward. Just the same, the thought of facing life alone was unbearable and in my shocked state it seemed the last straw that I'd been left to cope with his German Shepherd, Billie, who was three years old and about seven feet tall. On top of that she didn't think much of me.

Brook died at work. He left home after saying,

"Doug's picking me up today, so you and Clare can have the car." I didn't see him again. Not alive anyway.

I went to say goodbye to him at the funeral parlour and the person in the coffin didn't seem to be Brook. He looked very beautiful and I was surprised at the strength in his face, but he was so unlike the person I knew as Brook that the whole episode took on an air of unreality and I left the place with a feeling of relief because I thought Brook wasn't dead at all.

That night the dog crept onto my bed for comfort, and because I needed comfort too, I let her stay. After that, she always slept on the bed. She was so big she took up most of the room, but she did the best she could to make herself small. She seemed to fold herself up, and looking at her creamy chest and arched neck, I used to think she looked a little like a swan as she settled herself for the night.

We both waited for Brook to come home. Billie waited to hear his car coming around the corner. I waited to see his hand, with the little finger that had been broken and never set, come through the opening in the gate. We waited for him for almost a year.

While we waited I sometimes thought of the story Brook used to tell me about the wild geese. He got the story out of a book by Alan Watts. He carried the book around with him everywhere. In fact it had fallen to pieces and the pages were all separate, but he still carried it around in his pocket, and when he was out in the bush with Billie, he'd sit down somewhere and read it while she hunted.

I couldn't see the point of the story. It was about the Zen Master, Ma-tsu, who was out walking one day with a pupil. Some wild geese flew by and Ma-tsu asked Po-chang what they were. Po-chang told him. Ma-tsu then asked where they were going.

"They've already flown away," said Po-chang. Whereupon Ma-tsu grabbed his pupil by the nose and shouted at him, "How could they ever have flown away?" That's the end of the story. I couldn't see any meaning in it, but Brook liked it. He used to tease me about it and ask me sometimes, with a grin on his face, if I'd found out where the wild geese had gone. So I thought about it while I waited for him to come home, but of course he was dead and couldn't come home at all.

Towards the end of the year, Margot Blewitt, leader of the town's arty set, rang me.

"I'm having a smorgasbord luncheon on Sunday for the Art Train," she said. "I want you to come."

I asked her what the Art Train was.

Instead of answering me, she said, "You can't go on sitting at home grieving. It's unnatural. Your friends are beginning to worry about you. You must start going out. Meeting people. Life has a lot to offer you."

A chill rushed down my back. I remembered the shock of my mother shaking me after Brook's funeral and telling me that I was free to make a better marriage.

I put the memory firmly away and asked Margot again what the Art Train was.

Apparently I'd missed something because she said, "Pay attention, Vinnie. It's a thing some fool in the city dreamt up. A train is coming here for the weekend — each carriage, complete with tutor, will represent a branch of the graphic arts. We rustics, it seems, are to pay our dollar at one end and emerge twenty minutes later at the other as painters and potters."

I told her it sounded crazy to me and she said, "Of course it does, but all these important people are coming here and the least we can do is give them a decent lunch. I want you to come. It'll be good for you. I want you to get something new to wear and make this the start of a new life."

I said I'd think about it, but after I'd hung up the idea of a party appealed to me. God knows it was a long time since I'd been to one. If it came to that, it was a long time since I'd been anywhere at all. I didn't go out and I didn't see many people. Pandora Hunt was overseas and apart from Birdie Dadswell, the spinster from next door, the only adult visitor I had was Nicky Carr, a homosexual who lived in terror of some woman making a grab for his balls. He must have thought it over and decided he had nothing to fear at my place because he came around often with a little tin containing a mixture of tobacco and marijuana and he'd sit quietly and smoke on the veranda in the evenings.

I asked Billie how she felt about going to a party. The idea must have sounded good to her because she seized a plastic dish in her teeth, flew outside and tore round and round the lemon tree with it.

Having decided to go to the party, I thought I'd do it in style. I went to Maryston and at the shop where Hannibal bought all her denim gear, I bought a big hat of pale pink felt. When I got it home, I tied a poppy coloured scarf around it and decided that with the hat on my head and Billie at my heels, I'd steal the show at any smorgasbord.

The morning of the party, Margot telephoned me, "You won't bring Clare, will you? There won't be any children here."

"She didn't want to come. She's gone to a do at the ballet school."

"And you won't bring the dog, of course."

"Why not?"

"She's too big."

I thought of the look Billie would get on her face

when she found she was being left at home. "We can stay outside," I said. "We'd just as soon be outside."

"You can't stay outside. The whole point, Vinnie, is that I want you to come and mingle with people. You might as well stay at home as skulk in the garden." Having said that, Margot hung up.

I went to my bedroom and sat on the end of the bed. I looked at the hat which I had on display on a brass candlestick. For some reason I felt guilty. It was the kind of guilt I'd felt when I was ten and Irene threw our Mother's Day present at Bart and me. There'd been some kind of family row. As far as I know I wasn't involved in it, but looking at the box of soap on the floor I'd felt as guilty as hell. Hal must have given us the money for the soap. It was in a white box with a picture of a gardenia on the lid. I remember I'd ogled it for weeks in the chemist's shop before we bought it.

Billie interrupted my trip down misery lane by rushing in to see what I was doing. She stood looking at me in the manner of a dog who can't mind her own business. I gave her a push with my foot, but I might as well have tried to move Mount Kosciuszko. We stared at each other. The dog won. I got up, grabbed the hat, jammed it on my head and made for the door. Outside, I found it had begun to rain so I went to the laundry and got Brook's jacket — a garment with a ripped sleeve and a distinctly Ban-the-Bomb look.

We drove to my favourite place, Gooram Gooram Gong — the Valley of Singing Birds. In those days hardly anyone used to go there. Once I saw two nuns fishing in the pool below the falls. They had their robes tucked up and their feet in the water. Sometimes there'd be a man panning for gold, or a troop of boy scouts camping, but there were no kids with trail bikes and certainly no kids with automatic rifles.

39

Gooram Gooram Gong is a green and silver place. There's a creek which runs for a mile over gentle falls. Native trees and grass as tall as bamboo grow along its edges. The rocks in the creek are smooth and big enough to lie on. Above, the hill is covered with soft grass which bends when the wind blows and the whole of the hill turns silver. There are birds everywhere, wrens with bodies no more than an inch long and flocks of parrots in blues and greens and subtle reds.

We pottered over the rocks and through the grass for hours. Rain ruined my hat and I didn't care. Billie chased rabbits and once, after diving into the grass, came back to me with something in her mouth. I couldn't see what it was and told her to put it down. She didn't want to but in the end put a fieldmouse at my feet.

For a few moments the mouse, out of its mind with terror, stayed where it was then it shot away into the grass. I don't know why, but the mouse's dash for freedom lifted my depression. I sat down in the wet grass and laughed my first genuine laugh in months.

At the end of the day, turning the car to go home I hit a tree stump. The car jammed on top of it and we had to get out and walk for miles in the rain looking for help.

When I'd given up hope of meeting anyone, we found a couple mating like mad in the back of a station wagon. The boy was no more than fifteen; the girl was older, with a butch haircut and a spot of black decay forming a circle on her two front teeth. Both she and the boy went white when Billie stood up at the window to look at them. It took me some time to convince them she was harmless but in the end they took us back to our car and towed it off the stump.

The steering rods had been pushed out of line. On the way home the car kept veering to the right and we had to travel at twenty kilometres an hour, with the other motorists in their V8's cursing as they passed and some-times leaning out to shout obscenities. I didn't mind. I thought we'd had a good day and I turned to Billie to tell her so. She was exhausted from hunting and her tongue was lolling out. When I spoke she gave me a tipsy look from her kohl-rimmed eyes and I realised with a shock in my chest that we loved each other. That was the moment when I understood the story about the wild geese.

4

Life without Brook wasn't all picnics at Gooram Gooram Gong. Between his death and the time I reconciled myself to it, there were many dreadful days to get through. Some were worse than others, but the day his ashes arrived from the crematorium and the day I went to the compensation court in Melbourne were the worst of the lot.

I collected his ashes in Gorrangher at the sweet little red-brick post office where roses hang over the fence. Inside, the man who handed me the parcel was so embarrassed he couldn't look at me. While I was signing for it, he kept his eyes firmly on the wall behind my head.

The ashes were in a grey plastic box. I put it on the front seat of the car and drove to the place in the bush where I'd decided Brook would like to be. Apart from the box, I was alone and it was a weird feeling having it beside me. Brook was six foot two, the box was no more than eight inches. I felt as if I'd somehow got into a science fiction story and that if I spoke to the box it would answer me in an electronically controlled voice.

I didn't drive all the way to the place where I meant to leave the ashes. For some reason it seemed to me that it'd be disrespectful to Brook to arrive there by car, so I got out and walked the last mile into the bush. I had the box in one hand and a miner's hammer in the other.

It took me a long time to get the box open. The plastic was made to last. I managed in the end and scattered the ashes in the bush in a place where I thought I wouldn't mind being myself. It was among ironbarks on the top of a rise with a view of the mountains to the east. The day was hot and I couldn't hear any birds, but I knew they'd be there. I knew there'd be kangaroos too in the evenings.

People have told me since that you don't get the right person's ashes. That at the crematorium they put all the ashes in a pile and fill the plastic boxes with a shovel so that you get a mixture. Perhaps that's true. It makes sense. I don't think it matters much. At the time I was sure the ashes were Brook's and I did the best I could with them. I used to go now and then to the place where I put them and I always felt it was a good place to be. With the tall trees and the sudden whipping cry of birds it seemed to me to have the essence of the land which Brook loved perhaps more than he loved anything else.

I should be able to tell how I felt while I was scattering the ashes in the bush that day, but I can't. The point is that I didn't feel anything at all. I'd crossed the threshold to a place where there was nothing and that nothing was the worst feeling of all. I knew, though, that life would never be as bad again. In theory, at least, I'd be able to meet anything front-on and not give a damn. That was almost true, but not quite, for after that day, it took me a long time to learn to sleep quietly at night.

I thought the day of the compensation hearing would be one of the occasions when I'd be able to meet things front-on. I wasn't stupid enough to think it'd be pleasant. I knew it wouldn't be. When I'd done the business with Brook's ashes, at least I'd done it in private. The hearing would be in public and I'd already learnt how inquisitive people are about grief. More than that, I'd learnt that there are people who enjoy watching it. I decided the only way to handle the day would be to shut myself off and act, to act the part of a woman who'd been widowed too early. Up till that day, I fancied myself as an actress. When I was a child I didn't expect to be anything but an actress.

Once, when I was home from school with the mumps, Irene, who was a film fiend, dragged me off to a matinee of *Anthony Adverse*. She wound a woollen school scarf around my neck, dosed me with Aspros and took me there on the tram. I don't know whether I fainted or what, but the only thing I remember of the film was the gouty Duke's young wife slipping out of the chateau to meet her lover. She wore a crinoline with a cape over it, and her lover was dressed in what I thought were highwayman's clothes. They met beneath a huge tree and fell into each other's arms. I had no idea what lovers did after they'd kissed. As a child I was particularly naive about sex. I suppose I thought they collapsed into the sweet grass and swooned with bliss. Anyway, when I got over the mumps, I spent a lot of time acting out the scene from the film. I used to deck myself in one of Irene's evening dresses and a postman's blue serge cape which had somehow found its way into our laundry, then I'd rush into the garden and swoon as I met my lover. We didn't have the right kind of tree in our garden so I made do with the bougainvillea.

Irene told me that in the film the lover in the highwayman's clothes was run through with a sword by the Duke, so whenever I was tired of swooning with bliss, I acted out the scene of his death. It sounds as if I'm trying to be funny, but when I was a kid, I acted out those scenes with great seriousness, and in the weeks leading up to the court case, I was stupid enough to believe that all the rehearsing in childhood would help me through the real thing.

Brook was working for an American construction company engaged in putting bridges across the big irrigation channels in the Maryston Valley. The day he died, someone had left a live electric lead on the ground, and someone else had rolled a steel drum onto it. When Brook went on duty he grabbed the drum to move it out of the way and died as soon as he touched it.

His union had an inspector from the city at the site within two hours. He took statements from all of Brook's work-mates and then came to our house to tell me that the union would arrange and pay for a case against the construction company.

I had one meeting with my solicitor before the day of the case. He was a young Italian with a handsome pitted face and cynical eyes. We met again in the foyer of the Compensation Court in Bourke Street and before the lift shot us skywards, he told me Brook's employers had admitted liability and that the case wouldn't be defended.

The building was one of those windowless, air-conditioned places so high you feel you'll be on the moon when you reach the top. In fact, it was much as I've always imagined the headquarters of the CIA would be at Langley — muted voices, people scurrying about with files, and hanging over everything, an air of secrecy. On our way to the briefing room we passed several groups of people. In each there was an injured person, bandaged or in a wheelchair and looking as if they'd just returned from a hopeless mission. I remember thinking that in my borrowed clothes and with my world-weary escort I probably looked like a spy too.

For half an hour, Frank and I sat in a tiny airless room making embarrassed conversation while more of the walking wounded limped past the door. And that's where my acting career ended. The next part of the day was a blank. It must have been bad, for no matter how hard I tried at The Estuary, not one incident of the courtroom experience returned to me. I didn't even remember going *into* the courtroom, let alone what happened while I was there. I know I was the only woman present, but I guess I'd need to undergo hypnosis to remember the rest of it.

Later, I was on another level of the building talking to the registrar of the board. He told me that it was not his custom to see people immediately after their case, but that as I'd travelled a distance of two hundred kilometres, he'd decided to grant me an interview. Then he asked me what my assets were.

I asked him what he meant.

He must have thought I was trying to be funny, because his jaw muscles tightened and he said, "I'm trying to determine your financial position. Unless we can manage to do that today, you'll have to come back some other time. The court has awarded you the full amount of compensation to which Victorian law entitles you. You've been awarded thirty thousand, one hundred and twenty-seven dollars, but before we can advance any of it to you, we must determine your financial position."

I thought to myself that the sum of thirty thousand dollars was an incredibly small one in return for all the things that Brook had been. Four hundred million might have been nearer the mark. I sat thinking about it for a long time, and in the end I worked out that as the man who'd presided over the court had no way of knowing what Brook was worth to me, let alone to Clare, I had no right to hold the paucity of the sum against him.

The registrar was still speaking. He was saying, "Of course we don't give you the money. We hold it in trust and if you need part of it, you make application either by letter or by phone and the board considers your request."

I said, "I beg your pardon?"

By then the registrar had decided that he was dealing with an idiot. Patiently he explained that widows awarded compensation weren't allowed to handle the money in case they blew it on some doe-eyed fag. He didn't use those words, but that's what he meant.

I was appalled. I'd imagined myself going back down in the lift with the full four hundred million hanging out of my pockets.

When I didn't speak, the registrar said, "Of course it's a very old law. One day it'll be changed. But in some ways it works in your favour. When you're old enough to get the widow's pension, the moneys held in trust by us won't be taken into consideration, and when you remarry . . . "

I cut him off by saying, "I won't be remarrying."

He smiled and his face was flooded with Father-Knows-Best condescension. I knew he was about to tell me that of course I'd remarry and I knew too there was no point in telling him that I wouldn't, that when I'd married Brook, I'd married him for good, so instead, I said, "Your name's Butterfield, isn't it?"

He nodded, "Yes, Thomas Butterfield."

"The man who married us was called Butterfield too. That's funny, isn't it?"

I'd embarrassed him and he concentrated on the pile of forms lying on his blotter, so I told him quickly that my assets were a small weatherboard cottage in Gorrangher and a ten-year-old car. I told him how much money I had left in the bank and then I stood up and said goodbye and went out of his office.

47

Frank was waiting outside for me so we went to a pub near the court and had a beer and a sandwich. When we were sitting down I told him how I'd expected to leave the court with the pockets of Margot Blewitt's suit bulging with dollar bills.

He tried to find something sympathetic to say, "You'll marry again, you know."

Instead of arguing with him, I asked what had happened inside the courtroom.

For a moment he didn't know what I meant, and when he'd worked it out, he said, "Was it as bad as that?" I knew he didn't expect me to answer, so I waited and he went on. "We were only there a short time. The judge asked you if you could prove you were Brook's wife. You said, 'Yes', and handed the clerk of the court your marriage certificate. Then the judge asked if Brook had had any other dependants. Telling him you had a daughter, you passed over an extract of Clare's birth certificate.

"After that the young bloke who was representing Brook's employers stood up and told the court the company admitted liability and didn't wish to defend the case. Thereupon the judge told you you were entitled to full compensation."

I said, "If I were a man and I'd been awarded compensation for an injury, would they have given me the money or held it in trust?"

"You'd have got the money."

"A bit archaic, isn't it?"

"Yes, but remember that if you were a man whose wife had been killed at work, you'd have got nothing."

"That's even more archaic."

He smiled, "So don't bitch, eh?"

"Well, not at you," I said, and turned the talk to other things.

* * *

On the way back to Gorrangher that evening, the train was full of soldiers travelling to Puckapunyal. None of them looked to me to be more than twelve years old. The one sitting next to me was a bit pissed. He kept asking if I'd get out at Seymour with him and go to a dance.

I told him I was married, but he looked so much like Ritchie Cunningham in the television show "Happy Days", that I felt I knew him and as I spoke, I couldn't help laughing.

He waggled a finger at me and said, "Now, don't tell lies. You're not married. I know."

I asked him how he knew.

"Because the bloke who put you on the train at Spencer Street wasn't your husband."

"How do you know that?"

"I could tell by the way he was looking at you."

There was silence in the carriage as his mates waited to see what I'd say. They'd all stopped drinking to listen.

"No. He was my solicitor."

The boy beamed. "Then you're getting a divorce?"

"Something like that."

"So you can come to the dance with me."

"I can't y'know."

"Why not?"

"Because if I do, you'll be named as co-respondent."

He leaned back, nursed his beer can and tried to work out how much truth there was in my words. In the end the problem was too much for him and he said, "Mate, I *like* you."

Someone passed me a can and I started drinking too. My friend in the next seat didn't take his eyes off me, and every so often interrupted the conversation to ask again if I'd go to the dance. Finally, I agreed to dance with him in the corridor of the train.

Pissed or not, he danced like an angel. I'd expected

that we'd lurch around in the corridor like disco dancers, shooting our hips and looking cool. But it wasn't like that at all. As soon as we were out of the carriage he took me in his arms, and humming an Aznavour song, began to waltz. His body was young and boneless, he seemed scarcely to be holding me at all, but we melted together and danced as if we'd been dancing together all our lives. Neither the movement of the train nor its noise bothered Neil. He was a boy who could have done a breathtaking tango in a rowboat.

It seemed that we danced for hours. We danced together so easily that in the end he stopped humming and we just danced. We used the opened doorways of carriages for turns and sometimes we danced into carriages and out again. Each time we did that we were greeted by a cheer which came over us and vanished. I heard my skirt seam rip at the knee and danced on.

In the end, exhausted, I leaned against the window, and Neil, still holding me, leaned against me.

"Where did you learn to dance?" I gasped.

He said, "Where did you?" and he wasn't even out of breath.

"At school. Dancing school. I wanted to go on the stage."

"I learned at home with Mum. We used to dance every Friday and Saturday night. We had a lot of old records and a wind-up gramophone." As an afterthought he added, "My Dad's a cripple."

I was still out of breath. The train whistled. I knew we were close to Seymour. I moved my head to look out the window, but Neil stopped me by kissing me. It was a sweet, young, and to me, sexless kiss, but it went on for so long there in the rocking corridor that I suppose he came in his army underpants.

The train slowed. People began to push past us. Neil

50

put his chin on the top of my head, and still holding me said, "Will you come down to Seymour and dance with me?"

Knowing I never would, I said yes, and he let go of me and rushed back to the carriage for his beret and bag.

The evening train stops at Seymour for twenty minutes, so I got out with Neil and stood watching him as he went towards the gate with his mates. The rest of the crowd rushed to the cafeteria for tea and railway cake. At the archway he turned and saluted me, then he was gone.

It was dark by the time we pulled into Gorrangher. I'd tried to sleep after leaving Seymour, but too many images chased each other through my head and I hadn't been able to.

Hannibal met me at the station. She had a shocked look on her face which made me ask her what was wrong.

"When the train whistled, I was buying petrol," she said. "I backed out in a hurry and hit the bowser behind me. The side of the car's smashed in."

"Are you hurt?"

"No. I hit the passenger side."

Looking at her I realised she'd spent the evening blow-waving her hair and decorating her face so she'd look her best when I got off the train. We stood together on the bleak little railway platform with the battered Volkswagen on the other side of the wire fence and I remembered the time when she was seven years old and had looked out the east window of my house and said, "I love the railway station at night. I like the lights. They look exciting."

Exciting, for Christ's sake. The lights! There were five of them.

To find her waiting for me with what looked like an

entire bottle of Vegemite on her eyelashes, repaid me for a lot of the things that had happened that day. I wanted to tell her so, but instead I hit her softly with my bag and said, "It's like a movie, isn't it? Court cases, railway stations, smashed-up cars." Hannibal loved movies more than anything in the world. All the time when her mother was at work and thought Hannibal was at school, she was home instead watching old movies on television.

She laughed then and said, "You're a fool, Vinnie." But I knew she felt better and we went to her car and both crawled in through the driver's door.

As she started the engine, Hannibal sniffed and said, "You smell of beer."

I told her about the soldiers on the train and how one had asked me to dance with him.

We were already travelling on the dirt road towards my place, but Hannibal turned to gape at me. She still loved Brook and she meant to go on loving him, I'm sure, for the rest of her life. While she was gaping at me, we hit the railway track where it crossed the road. It took her a few moments to get the Volkswagen under control. When she did, she said, "You kissed him, didn't you?"

It was my turn to gape. "How did you know?"

"You kiss everybody. When you get pissed, you'd kiss a horse."

"Oh come on, for Christ's sake. I don't *know* anyone — let alone kiss them."

"You find them."

"I guess I'm one of the Great Kissers of the World," I said, referring to an old joke of ours.

She didn't answer, and I said, "It wasn't anything. He was only a kid. If you want to know, it was like kissing Christopher Robin."

She took the corner near my house as if she was leading the field at Le Mans. The car lights picked up Billie waiting at the gate. As we shot towards her, she leapt for her life, then we flew into the drive and skidded to a halt under the pergola.

Hannibal cut the motor and switched off the lights. "Listen," I said, "sometimes things get out of hand. Today was like that."

She thought about it while Billie scrabbled at the door. Finally she said, "Okay, but I don't want to talk about it," and got out of the car.

As I climbed out through the driver's door, Billie grabbed my bag and ran into the orchard with it. Hannibal chased her and in a second they'd both vanished in the dark. I went alone into the house. The light was on in the back hall and the first thing I saw was a huntsman spider clinging to the Chinese wall-hanging. Right in the centre of it as if he'd been embroidered there. He was the biggest spider I'd seen and must have spanned five inches. He was a soft cocoa colour with a slightly paler head and his eyes were black. I went close and stared at him. He watched me. I knew he was thinking, "Friend or foe?" and that his legs which could run at a hundred kilometres an hour were ready to move. Before he knew what I was doing, I'd snatched off my shoe and hit him. He fell on his back on the floor with most of his legs already folded on his belly. One leg remained straight. The leg twitched twice and I thought, "God, he's going to die slowly. I'll have to hit him again," but with what seemed to me exquisite grace, he folded the leg so that it formed a pattern with the others on his belly. Then he was still.

I was horrified at what I'd done. I stooped and picked him up in my hand. In death he was tiny, made of velvet like some exotic seed pod. I wanted him to be alive again

and fast and menacing. Without warning the dam inside
me broke. The tears I hadn't cried when Brook died
came and I cried as I'd never cried in my life before. And
Hannibal came in and stood beside me and didn't know
what to do.

5

After the court hearing I spent a few months hanging around the house and orchard like a ghost, then lack of money made me take a job in Maryston. I went to work at the branch office of an old-fashioned, Melbourne-based firm of accountants where my duties included typing tax returns and totalling ledgers without the help of a machine. Mr Strauss, the manager, was a withered old man with courtly manners and radiant false teeth. For me the compensation was that he spent his afternoons over at the Grand, conducting the firm's business there in the saloon bar. My work was often finished by three thirty and after that I'd write what I hoped were snappy little stories and poems which I didn't show to anyone.

I'd been there only ten weeks when Mr Strauss had a stroke and had to retire. When that happened another withered old man, this time with lemon peel skin and a superbly tailored suit, came from Melbourne to ask me if I minded holding the fort until they found a new manager. Imagining myself alone all day working on my secret little stories, I hastened to say yes. But things didn't work out that way. I soon found myself filling in tax returns as well as typing them and when the directors in Melbourne realised the work was being done on a typist's pay, they left me to get on with it. Whether or not they tried to find a manager, I don't know, but none turned up and I was there alone for the next four years.

Apart from the loss of freedom, the hardest part of being at work was keeping up with the acre of garden at home. It became impossible and that's how I met Beauregard. He followed the string of loons who came to mow the grass for me. The first of these loons was a gambler who had a big win one Saturday and left town without letting anyone know. The next sprayed my hedge with poison because it gave him asthma. The hedge survived but the spray killed my favourite cat.

After the hedge poisoner there was Weird Al, who'd advertised himself for hire in the local paper as a relief milker and part-time gardener. I answered his advertisement and three weeks later on a Sunday, he turned up wearing a crumpled black suit and shoestring tie. I suppose he'd been at church. Just the sight of him frightened me. He had a small head, enormous ears and hands like catchers' gloves. Not game to take him inside I sat with him on the veranda and during the interview which followed he kept leaping to his feet to shake my hand. Altogether he shook it four times.

In spite of the doubts I had about his gardening ability, I arranged for him to start on my lawns the next day. I also arranged for him to call on a friend of mine who lived nearby and wanted her lawns cut too. After another round of handshakes at the gate he left and didn't come back. He went to Wendy's though.

He called at her place when she was at work. Wendy's a child psychologist and in those days was running a day-centre for emotionally disturbed children. Her own children were left at home with the housekeeper and ran around all summer without their clothes because Wendy thought it a healthy thing for them to do. When Weird Al called they were naked and the housekeeper had gone next door for coffee. From the wild stories I heard later, Al had a wonderful time. He took the six-year-old girl into the lavatory and locked the door. Among other things he peed all over the walls.

By the time Wendy got home, the housekeeper had rescued the child and got rid of Al, but the damage had been done. The next time they had a dinner party the child asked in front of the guests when was Big Al coming back for some more games in the loo. The reaction she got was so momentous, she started asking the same question every time they had visitors. When Wendy trapped me in the supermarket and told me she was reduced to locking the child in her room whenever anyone called at their house, I murmured, "So much for child psychology," and what with one thing and another our friendship wasn't the same after Weird Al passed through our lives.

Beauregard, when he appeared, was like a gift from heaven. By that time I was so desperate for help, I'd advertised in the local paper too. Beau answered. He loped into my office in Maryston wearing a tee shirt with a picture of a man in a Kendo suit on it wielding a rake instead of a staff.

In a deep musical voice he said, "You advertised, Madam?" Then he dazzled me with his smile.

He wasn't just handsome, he was beautiful. He was six foot three with black hair, blue eyes and that *smile*. He wore steel-framed spectacles which had one sidepiece missing and he had an endearing habit of adjusting them every so often. I was fascinated by him.

I think he liked working at my place because he always came to do the lawns in the evenings when I was at home. As things turned out he didn't do much work. Instead we used to sit with our feet on the kitchen table, drink beer and talk. Beau was a Black Belt karate man, and as if that wasn't interesting enough, he was writing a book about some chap who'd spent his life researching the myths of Australian Aborigines. The man's surname was the same as mine but that's all I know about him. (In those days I didn't listen to Beau much, I just drank my beer and looked at him.)

In the summer months we sat on the back steps instead of at the kitchen table, and under a sky famous for its night-time luminosity, we'd discuss such philosophical subjects as whether or not animals had souls.

My argument was that as people didn't have them, neither did animals. Beau said he was certain people had souls and I told him in that case animals had them too.

"What about ants?" said Beau.

At that stage Charlotte, the girl Beau lived with, rang up and asked when he was coming home. I didn't ever meet her. She was pregnant and apparently shy. According to Beau, she was a painter but too shy to show her stuff to anyone. As I said, we didn't meet, but we talked often on the phone. I suppose you could say we talked to each other almost every time Beau came to mow my lawns.

About an hour after she'd rung, Beau would go home and whether he'd finished the lawns or not, he was always careful to pick up his money from the kitchen table. (He told me that most people leave the gardener's money under the rubbish bin, which seems to me a tasteless sort of thing to do.)

Beau was full of get-rich-quick schemes. Not only did he want to be rich, he wanted to be famous as well. He spoke of it so often it was clearly an obsession and when I heard his history, I could see why. The eldest of five children, he was born in England and when he was eight his father died.

"My mother was a widow," he said and keeping his eyes on mine, added, "a real one."

The implication that I was a sham widow made me laugh. Beau didn't respond to my laughter, just went on with his story. The family had emigrated to Australia when he was nine. They'd lived in various bush towns and apparently had a tough time. To supplement the widow's pension, Beau's mother had worked as a cleaner. Listening to Beau talk about her, it became obvious that silk shirts and champagne weren't the only things he wanted. He also wanted the esteem of the people who'd looked down on his mother when she cleaned their houses.

He'd grown up wearing hand-me-downs, and because he'd grown quickly some of the hand-me-downs had been ridiculous on him. At school one day he took to the football field in a pair of women's boots — light tan ones. When the coach saw them he ordered Beau back to the dressing room. Leaving the field to the laughter of his peers, Beau decided to find a different world to live in.

He'd noticed that there was one man admired by the entire population of the town — Mardy Sparkes, who owned the local gym and taught karate. Beau went to see him and offered to clean the gym in return for lessons.

Mardy was a funny-looking fat guy with a wispy moustache. He stared long and hard at Beau, then walked around him in a circle.

Finally he said, "Why do you want to learn?"

Beau knew he was required to say something wise and Zen-like, but couldn't think of a thing. In desperation he blurted, "I've got no choice. I had to play football in women's boots."

Mardy threw back his head and let go with a big "Ho, ho." Then he said, "We'd better teach you to do it with poise then, hadn't we? Come tomorrow after school.

59

You needn't do the cleaning. Learn Karate-Do, learn it well. That will pay me."

So Beau was on his way. By the time he left school, he was a Black Belt, First Dan. He could wear anything he liked on his feet and no one laughed at him.

Somewhere along the line Mardy and Beau had a row. It was so bad it caused Beau to leave home and come to the Maryston Valley. What it was about, I didn't ever find out. But Beau was a handsome boy and I've always suspected it involved Mardy's wife. On the few occasions I asked Beau about it, he shut up like a clam and went home, so I learned not to ask.

Beau often gave me little lectures on karate. "In fighting an opponent," he'd say, "you're really fighting to get rid of your own ego. Because ego's the thing that limits us." Then he'd toss in a quotation from some Japanese master to back the statement up. At other times he'd demonstrate breathing techniques or show me how to maintain a correct posture. From there we progressed to what he called fighting blocks and grips.

I enjoyed those sessions, telling myself that as Clare and I lived alone it was good for me to know the elements of self-defence. In reality what I enjoyed was Beau's company with its saucing of physical contact.

In the Maryston Valley there's a week in October when everything in the garden blooms in one primal burst. It was during such a week that Beau chose to show me how to apply a wrist lock. We were standing on the back lawn with Beau holding my arm when I interrupted the lesson to say, "Listen! In the grape vine. It's the scissor grinder." I tried to imitate the strange whirring call of the bird and failing, laughed and added, "It turns up about this time every year."

Beau's response was to bend his head and kiss me. He smelt of something like wattle, and male sweat and fresh-cut grass so that the kiss became an extraordinarily complete experience as if the spring night itself and I had fused. When our mouths parted we stood looking at each other and although I knew I should break the spell by making some banal comment, I couldn't. It was broken when Clare came flying from the house to say, "Beau, Charlotte just rang. She wants you to go home and take her shopping."

"Damn Charlotte," said Beau softly.

"I expect she's tired of being alone all day," I told him. "You can't blame her for that."

"No, I can't." He let go of my arm and turned and went to the place where he'd left his things.

Watching him go I had the sense to realise that an affair with a good-as-married karate-practising gardener eight years my junior was something I was in no state to handle and although I maintained my friendship with Beau, from then on when he called I kept a cooling edge on my voice — my behaviour too. At that time he may not have been sophisticated enough to know what prompted my signals but he read them correctly and there were no more karate lessons on my back lawn.

At the end of summer I arrived home one day to find him cutting the front hedge. He called something to me as I turned into the drive but being hot and out-of-sorts I kept going. After parking in the shade I went inside, dumped my parcels and rummaged in the fridge for something to drink. Beau came in as I was opening a bottle of cider.

"That's stuff's lethal," he said.

"I feel lethal."

"I guessed as much when I saw you come in. A bad day?"

"Frightful. One of the bosses came from Melbourne and I had to be his handmaiden instead of getting on with my work. The awful part is that I found myself running around with cups of coffee and agreeing with every bit of bullshit he spouted."

"Forget about it — we'll soon be rotten-rich and away from here."

"Oh yes?" I drowned my mouth in cider.

"I mean it. I've finally hit on a plan to make a million and it's simple enough to work."

I pushed a glass across the table to him. "I'm listening."

"I'm going to launch a travelling show of the martial arts. We'll do two nights here to get some capital, then tour Australia. We'll make a mint. People are hot for it — Karate-Do, Wing Chun, Kendo, Kyudo — we'll do the lot. It can't miss."

I sat down and took my time thinking about the plan. After a while I said, "Who's going to do all this? You and Charlotte and the baby?"

Beau laughted. "I've already worked that out. I can get three other blokes. There's Chinka Sloane, who does Kendo . . . "

"The Way of the Sword."

Delighted that I'd remembered, Beau lifted his glass to me. "Another mate, Graham Fenn does Wing Chun."

"What's that, pray?"

"It's a form of karate known as the sticky hands method and was evolved by a Buddhist nun." He peered at me over his spectacles. "You'll like him — Charlotte does. She thinks he's very good looking. And there's another guy, Pete Neilson, who's an archer. He's superb. He looks directly in front of himself and shoots at a target at right angles to his line of vision." Beau mimed the action.

By then the cider had begun to affect me and when he said, "I want you to take care of the business side of things — do the books, look after the money and so on. Will you?" I laughed and said yes. And I went on listening to his plans, adding to them in fact until Clare came in to ask if there was going to be any dinner that night.

It turned out that Beau's scheme was no pipedream. To my surprise the show went on and was a smashing success, running for three nights in Maryston and one in Gorrangher as well. I think everyone in the district went, even Mike Duffield, who'd told me more than once that he found my interest in the martial arts offensive.

I looked after the tickets and money as Beauregard had asked and on the last night when we'd counted everything, we celebrated with champagne instead of cider.

After the party when the others had gone home, Beau and I sat on the back step. At first we didn't speak, just sat in silence while a small breeze moved through the garden. Then Beau said, "We've made enough — more than enough — to go on tour. We can go straightaway. There's nothing to stop us."

When I didn't answer, he said, "You'll come, won't you?"

"No. No, I guess I won't."

"Why not?"

"Well, there's not just me, is there?"

"Of course not, but Clare can come too. She'll learn as much by travelling as she would at school and anyway, she can do lessons by correspondence."

"She wouldn't leave her ballet class, let alone Mrs Curno."

"She would if you made her."

Again I didn't answer and Beau said, "Is it because of that chap Duffield?"

Surprised that Beau knew so much about me, I said, "No, it's not because of him. I have a comfortable little affair with him, that's all."

Watching me, Beau adjusted his glasses before saying, "I wouldn't have picked him as your type."

"He's not. That's why it's comfortable."

Beau gave himself time to work that out, then said, "There's more to life, surely, than being comfortable."

I giggled. "Not for me. I like the little things, like the souls of ants."

"Even an ant would know when to stop mourning."

Taken aback by his perspicacity, I murmured, "Maybe so, but in my case it boils down to this — there are things here I'm simply not ready to leave."

"Such as?"

"The garden. The sagging old garage where Brook left his car."

I expected Beau to counter with some Eastern adage about the left nostril of Buddha, but all he did was say, "I understand." Then he stood, said goodnight quietly and went home.

A few days later he left town with Charlotte and the troupe. During the next two years I heard from him regularly. Sometimes he sent notes, sometimes letters. One letter was forty-seven pages long. In writing it, he'd used up an entire writing pad and overflowed onto some Walt Disney paper with cartoon characters in the corners. They were wonderful letters. He described cities, towns, the countryside and the people he met along the way. He described them well. I'd like to quote some bits here but because I believe Beau wrote the letters for himself as much as for me and that one day he'll turn them into a damned good book, I'm not going to. I kept them though, filed in date order and tied with a piece of silk cord. I kept them in a shoebox in the corner of my wardrobe.

Charlotte was still with Beau, still painting, probably still shy. She had a second child and although they were in Darwin when it was born, she had the manners not to give it an Aboriginal name.

Then the letters stopped. They didn't taper off, they stopped in midstream as it were. At first I thought something had happened to Beau, but no news of an accident or illness reached me and I didn't know what to think. My letters to him were returned unclaimed. I guess six or seven months went by with no news of Beau at all.

Just before Christmas that year I asked the boss at head office for a day off and went to Melbourne by train to do some shopping. The train left early in the morning and I walked to the station before anyone was about. The air was full of butterflies. Three years before, a lot of orchardists had bulldozed their trees, pushed them into piles and burnt them. All through the winter the sky had been hazy with smoke. The government paid the orchardists to get rid of their trees, which was pretty funny because it had paid them to come and plant them in the first place.

When the orchards were there, the bees and birds and butterflies went away or died. Mostly they died because of the poisons the orchardists sprayed in the air. Slowly, after so many of the trees were burnt, they started to come back. That morning when I was walking to the station they were everywhere and I thought to myself how beautiful the world must have been before man got loose.

Billie climbed onto the train with me. I got her off with the help of the guard and a small boy. Afterwards the boy sat near me and every time I caught his eye, he beamed at me as if we'd served overseas together in a war.

It took a long time to reach the outskirts of the city, then we crept at a snail's pace through the suburbs. I was half asleep at the window when suddenly I saw a billboard looming out the sky. On it was a gigantic picture of Beauregard. His glasses had gone and he was wearing a gold karate suit trimmed with black. He looked stunning. The billboard advertised a film called *Ku Fu Glory* and Beau was its star. I wanted to get off the train and run back and gaze at the billboard. That wasn't necessary because I saw another two before we pulled into Spencer Street.

My imagination hadn't run riot. Beau *had* made a film and instead of going shopping I went to see it. It was pretty bad — a weak story strung together with wild action. Love triumphed in the final leap and close-up. The audience loved it, obviously loved Beau too. He had star quality. There was no doubt about that. No matter how many people were on the screen, you looked at Beau, no matter how beautiful the Hong Kong heroine was, you looked at Beau. You couldn't help yourself.

I travelled home that night delighted by Beau's success. At the same time I felt a little nag of sadness because he'd sailed so far from my orbit.

To my surprise, in a couple of months the letters started again. I learned then how Beau got into movies. For some reason, the martial arts troupe had folded in the Northern Territory. Beau had looked around for something else to do and had decided to open a lion park. He'd had to pull a lot of strings to get it going, but by then he'd had the money to do it. Not long after the park opened, it was visited by an Italian film director and his spunky young wife. The young wife took one look at Beau and before he knew it, he was on his way to Spain and stardom. Charlotte didn't go with him. Beau didn't say why and I didn't ask. I didn't worry much about her though. Girls as shy as Charlotte seldom have trouble finding someone to take them in. It seems that in Charlotte's case this was true because I later

66

heard she'd married Graham Fenn and taken over the lion park.

As for Beau, he made more movies — all of them bad, all of them financial successes. My friends gave me hell about him. And Duffield, convinced that an airline ticket would arrive for me any day in the mail, put on a pout I didn't know he possessed. He needn't have worried; no ticket came and anyway I was content to stay in the Maryston Valley enjoying Beau's career from afar.

He turned up in all sorts of places — in the glossies dining with creamy starlets at Cannes, on cards in the breakfast cereal packets. Sometimes he sent presents. I'd get a batch within a few days of each other, then there'd be nothing for months. They ranged from a Samurai sword to a collection of hairpins made of jade. The accompanying letters were as good as the earlier ones had been; slow descriptions of life in other countries and fast funny gossip of the movie world.

Beau made two more films, then he disappeared again and the letters stopped. I heard nothing of him at all until I opened the paper one Saturday and found an article about him. It said he'd turned his back on the good life and gone to Korea to study and meditate.

There are friendships which run their course and end and I told myself that ours had been one of them. Nevertheless, I kept his letters. From time to time Duffield would ask me if I'd got rid of them and I always said, "No, but I'm going to." Somehow I didn't get around to doing it and when I finally moved, I got them out and read them again. Then I put them in one of my suitcases, shoebox and all, and took them to Queensland with me.

CLARE

6

I'd begun to write a series of stories about my great-aunt Helen. There was plenty to say about her. In her youth she'd been a suffragette and later, during the course of a career as a balloonist in California, she'd had some startling adventures.

My main reason for writing about Helen Seymour was to keep my mind away from the subject of my daughter, Clare. It wasn't easy to avoid thinking about her. For one thing her cat was living with me and there were other things about the house to remind me of her when I least expected it. A snapshot would fall from one of Irene's books and suddenly Clare's face would be on the floor looking up at me.

On the whole I was pleased with my new life and what I thought of as the new Vinnie, but one day at the beach the lot of it was undone by the sight of a child doing clumsy pirouettes while damp sand fell from the seat of her bathers. Immediately I was back in the garden at Gorrangher where Clare, aged seven, was twirling across the grass into shadow and out of it again.

Clare was a tall child with her father's colouring and big eyes. In those days she and I spent almost all our time together and looking back it was easy to see that I'd have been wise to cultivate some other interests. My only outside occupation was going in the summer months to watch Brook play cricket with the local team. I even jibbed when Birdie Dadswell asked us to join the Art Appreciation Society in Maryston. I felt I knew exactly what the meetings would be like — farmers and doctors' wives saying that most of the stuff written and painted since the turn of the century wasn't art at all. It's doubtful that Brook, with his taste for the avant-garde, enjoyed going but he had a lot of time for Birdie and went anyway.

Clare and I stayed at home, working on her bits of homework and making up dance steps in the sunroom. I suppose it's true to say of that time that I was enjoying the last dazzle of my own childhood. Certainly I was unaware that changes were inevitable.

A few weeks after Clare's eighth birthday, Brook came home from a meeting to say he'd run into someone called Panni Abbott. At first I thought he was talking about some sort of Indian priest but it turned out that Pandora Hunt, née Abbott, was a schoolfriend he hadn't seen for twenty years. She and her husband had just moved to the district to take up jobs at the high school and in order to introduce herself socially, Pandora had joined the Art Appreciation Society.

Interrupting himself at one stage to put out a bee he'd found trapped inside the window, Brook talked of Pandora and his schooldays until I realised that in whisking me away from my parents, he'd cut himself off from his own past as well. Not only that, but he missed that past and had probably done so for years.

The next weekend we dined with the Hunts. They lived ten miles out of Maryston in a long brick house half hidden by the shoulder of the road. To reach it we had to leave the car and climb down a series of steps. The house was to the left of them with a terrace and a narrow strip of garden in front. Beyond it was a little valley full of willow trees and smoky shadows. Halfway down we stopped to admire the view and by the time we'd reached the bottom step, Pandora had slid open a window of the house and come onto the terrace to meet us.

After greeting Brook, she turned her attention to me, staring boldly, almost blatantly.

"Yes," she said, "you're just right," and scarcely taking her eyes from me, she snapped off a geranium head from a bush nearby and before I realised what she intended doing, she'd advanced on me and tucked it into my belt. Then, while I could still feel where her fingers had busied themselves at my waist, she stepped back and said, "There, now you're perfect."

For some reason I felt unsure of myself and didn't answer; it didn't matter because Brook was being poetic about the view and Pandora was bending over Clare to introduce herself. I took time then to study her, although it wasn't necessary because my mind had registered all the things I needed to know about her earlier when she'd opened the window and stepped out.

Of Brook's age, thirty-eight, she was a short woman with smooth dark hair gathered up into a knot. She had big round breasts and big round eyes and a mouth which seemed to be at odds with so many circles. It was a long mouth, a cat's mouth, with a little vertical groove at each end like another opening. The scanner inside my head had also noted and filed facts about her Indian dress of blues and purples and the way she planted her feet firmly, almost aggressively on the ground.

Deciding there was little chance of her snatching Brook away from me, I relaxed and began to look around the garden. Pandora kept us outside for a few more minutes, then took us into the house. The room we entered was at least fifty feet long with a grand piano in it and a telescope mounted on a tripod. There were two thronelike chairs of leather and wood in front of a television set and to one side a jumbled collection of others. Books were everywhere and on one wall was an abstract painting with a great deal of violence in it. Later I was surprised to learn that it was Pandora's work. At the other end of the room, next to a refectory table, were two English-looking bikes, a motor-mower and a set of golf clubs.

Pandora told us her husband Kim was in his study working on a thesis to do with the influence of Gaelic poetry on the politics of Ireland. He didn't appear until food was on the table and the rest of us were seated. For me, at least, he was something of a surprise, a small man some years younger than Pandora, with a thin boyish face beneath a mop of grey-streaked hair. He had on khaki fatigues and was carrying two bottles of home-made wine.

"Parsnip," he told us, bobbing around the table to pour it.

Brook gave me a look so still, I knew he wanted to laugh, but the wine too was a surprise, delicate and dry with a pleasant aftertaste. As for the food, from vichyssoise to tarts of wine and peaches, it was a triumph for Pandora.

One of my strongest memories of that night is of Pandora's hands fluttering about the table like a pair of pale excited birds. She used them constantly when talking and she talked almost all the time. Now and then she fed her husband a good line the way a mother does with a bright child but for the most part the rest of us listened while she gave us a detailed history of her life since she and Brook last met.

Late in the evening when Clare, grown tired, left her chair and came to lean against me I thought I saw Pandora watching us with a look of hunger on her face. Almost immediately she moved her head and the look was gone.

We left the Hunts that night full of good fellowship. After that we dined with them at least once a month, and whether at our place or theirs the evenings followed the same pattern with Pandora talking and the rest of us listening.

I used to see her in between the dinners too because although she was by far the busiest person I knew, she found time after school to call on me with presents of brandied fruit and Jugoslavian jam. She'd stay only a few minutes, smoke half a cigarette, tell me that a pile of Kim's typing was waiting at home to be done, then kiss my cheek and leave. In one way and another Pandora did a lot of Kim's work for him including most of the research and even some of the thesis itself. And always when I saw them together, I was reminded of a mother promoting an unusually clever child.

Pandora obviously liked children and she had a good relationship with Clare. She didn't seem to go out of her way to achieve it, but perhaps because she was a teacher she seemed to know exactly what pleased my daughter. In her bedroom there was a trunk of her grandmother's clothes and geegaws and she was always ready to let Clare dress up in them. Clare loved that and on the few occasions when Brook and I went somewhere without her, she accepted our absence cheerfully as long as we arranged for her to stay with the Hunts.

Soon after we met him, Kim Hunt made two trips to Ireland to do research for his thesis. The first time, Pandora went with him but on the second trip he went alone; I don't know why because neither of the Hunts offered an explanation. In his absence Pandora busied herself in arranging picnics and lunch parties. Sometimes Hannibal was included in our invitation but not often. For some reason Pandora didn't take to her and asked me once if I thought it wise for me to let a girl of thirteen follow Brook all over the place. When I answered straight-faced that any child who'd recognised Brook's worth as Hannibal had done was almost certainly the reincarnation of some Tibetan monk and entitled to privileges, Pandora held my gaze boldly for a few moments then changed the subject.

Clare was almost nine when a Russian woman, Katy Curno, opened a school of ballet in Maryston. I think my daughter was the first to enrol. She'd always been keen on ballet, or at least the idea of it. Like many girls of similar age she had photographs of ballerinas tacked up in her room and she was forever asking me to show her dance steps. I must admit that for someone without any knowledge of dance technique she managed to float and spin with a surprising amount of grace.

The morning she enrolled with Mrs Curno, she was nervous for the first time in her life. In the car on the way to Maryston I realised *how* nervous and reached for her hand but she disengaged it almost immediately and in doing so, let me know that she was about to enter a world where I would not be needed.

From the first lesson, her obsession with ballet worried me. When I said as much to Brook, he told me I was suffering a second set of labour pains, but remembering my own high-spirited bursts of tap-dancing, I found Clare's dedication to the discipline unnatural. She spoke of nothing else and before long had begun to set the alarm at five thirty in order to do an hour's practice before leaving for school. When that happened, I went to see Mrs Curno and pointed out that Clare was only a little girl.

With a roll of her Russian eyes, Mrs Curno said, "Ah

yes — a little girl indeed but one made of spring steel which needs stretching like this." And she put her hands together then whipped them apart.

I started to protest but realising that Mrs Curno and I would never see eye to eye where my daughter was concerned, I said goodbye instead.

At ten, Clare danced briefly and I must say charmingly, at the school's midyear concert but to me the trancelike look on her face was disturbing and I turned to Pandora who was next to me and said so.

It was the opportunity Pandora had been waiting for. Without taking her eyes from the stage, she said, "She's probably the reincarnation of Pavlova."

When I recounted the episode to Brook, he saw only the funny side of it and after that, more or less giving up, I let the dancer have her head.

Our little family was intact for another eighteen months and then Brook died. I've already told how crazy I went, how I waited for almost a year for him to come home, but I haven't told about the first three weeks of that year, the weeks when I ignored my beautiful child. At a time when she needed desperately to be held and comforted, I let my own grief blind me to hers, let her get most of her own meals, find what clean clothes she could and get herself to school. It's not as if I didn't know what I was doing — I did. But I don't think I cared, I was too busy trying to come to terms with my introduction to death. Nothing had prepared me for the shock I got when I was suddenly face to face with the fact that fruit and trees and birds and people, Clare and I included, must all die and decompose. I'd known it, I suppose in a superficial way, but I hadn't thought about it, certainly hadn't tried to weave it into my philosophy. Then crack! There it was in front of me and I knew that being alive was just a fearful joke. After that, how could

I comfort my daughter when I had no comfort to give?

Then, one night on my way to bed, I passed her room and saw she'd fallen asleep with the light on. Pausing to switch it off, I saw the cat asleep on the bed and Clare's hand clutching a fistful of its fur. The sight of that desperate little hand brought me to my senses. Horrified at what I'd done, I began to tidy her room. From then on I tried to make amends, but it was too late. The shock of her father's death, followed by my rejection of her, had driven Clare into some chill refuge whose walls I couldn't breach, and she turned aside each overture I made with politeness and a marble face.

When that had gone on for some weeks, I should have sought professional help. Instead I turned to Pandora. She'd been extremely kind to both of us, taking charge of the funeral arrangements and other things as well. To ask her advice about Clare seemed the natural thing to do and when I did, she said, "You worry too much. Clare's suffering grief of course but she's also having growing pains and there are times, Vinnie, when you tend to smother her. Stand back a little and let her breathe."

It was nonsense but nonsense spoken so authoritatively I believed it and am ashamed to say I let things go on the way they were until November.

During that period my own behaviour was far from normal. I knew death existed, acknowledged the fact inside my head but still I went on watching the gate for Brook. No doubt Clare's big grey eyes saw all of that, certainly there were times I'd catch her watching me above her homework and when that happened, I'd make some excuse and leave the room.

I've told too how Brook's dog, Billie, made me see the point of the story about the wild geese, showed me that something once experienced can never be lost. The lesson allowed me to fit death into the scheme of things and looking around me, I decided that if life was a joke, it was a sublime one and should be treated as such. My love for Clare resurfaced, but it had a new dimension because as her father had done I was able to love her as a person instead of an extension of myself.

The change in me heralded another — Hannibal came back. She'd stayed away since the day Brook died. I'd been glad of that. She'd been so much Brook's girl that I didn't want to see her and I suppose she felt the same about me.

We didn't have a tearful and dramatic reunion. She was simply there one morning when I got home from a visit to the dentist. She was sitting cross-legged beneath the willow tree and almost hidden by its waterfall of foliage. If she hadn't had a bright shirt on, I doubt that I'd have seen her. She was using a twig to make a pattern on the ground and when I cycled in the gate, didn't hear me until I pulled up and said, "Are you going to invite me into your willow tent?"

Looking up, she hesitated then smiled and said, "Yes, but there's no homemade ginger beer this time."

That oblique reference was the only one we made to the past but having acknowledged it to each other's satisfaction, we more or less took up where we'd left off. There was a difference though because it turned out that Hannibal had recently met a rally driver, Alan Weston, and fallen heavily for his smooth dark skin and splendid nutcracker teeth. A lot of her time was being spent in helping him take his car apart and in accompanying him to rallies in different parts of the country.

Alan came from a well-established farming family and although his conversation seemed to consist of one-syllable replies, he was easygoing and laughed a lot. There's no doubt that he was good for Hannibal — indeed when I saw them together, I was bowled over by the happiness on her face.

I must admit that having found Hannibal again, I missed her furiously when she was away with Alan. Nevertheless I was glad that she'd managed to resolve the problem of Brook's absence in such a normal and satisfactory manner.

At that time I kept hoping that Clare and I would have our equivalent of a reunion under the willow tree. It didn't happen. My daughter, more ballet-minded than ever, came and went with the chill dreaminess of someone already distanced by the orchestra pit and footlights. At home she spent most of her time in her room and although I went on making overtures whenever I got the chance, her response remained at the level of "Do you think I could have four dollars for my geography project?"

More than once I asked myself if Clare, who seemed to have no friends of her own age, could be jealous of my relationship with Hannibal, but remembering the way her eyes lit up at some of Hannibal's saltier remarks and the way she'd search Maryston for the perfect present each time her birthday came around, I'd be satisfied that my daughter's life, like mine, was warmed by Hannibal's presence and seasoned by her sense of humour.

As for Pandora Hunt, her relationship with Clare was as good as ever. She'd ring now and then to pass on Mrs Curno's compliments and in answering her, Clare would be as cheerful and easygoing as any other girl. On top of that, although Clare disliked being driven anywhere by me, she was always pleased to get a lift with Pandora and it was surprising to see how often Pandora was going in the right direction.

7

Clare turned thirteen in April and in the holidays that followed, Kim Hunt went to Ireland again. I was still working in Maryston and when Pandora offered to have Clare each day, I agreed.

The arrangement was a successful one and when Pandora dropped her back at home the day before school started we decided to do the same thing in the September holidays. Pandora left, tooting her car horn cheerfully at the end of the drive but to my surprise, two days later she was back again.

It was eight thirty in the morning and as I rushed from the bedroom with my car keys in my hand I met Pandora in the hall. She had a scarf tied gypsy-fashion on her head and for some reason had drawn big dark eyebrows on herself. Altogether she looked like someone done up to do crystal-gazing at a fete.

Smothering a laugh, I said, "You've missed Clare — she's gone on the bus."

"It's you I want to see." Pandora's voice was so low I had to guess at the words. Then she cleared her throat and spoke more distinctly. "Could we sit somewhere?"

"Of course — in here." I waved her into the sitting room.

With a step heavier than usual, Pandora went past me

and ignoring more comfortable chairs, squashed herself into the piano seat.

I knew then she'd had some kind of shock and as gently as I could said, "Shall I make coffee?"

I don't think Pandora heard me because instead of answering she locked her eyes on my face and said, "Kim's not coming back."

I said, "Shit," in a silly sort of way and Pandora, giving a tight little smile, said, "Exactly."

"Are you sure?"

"Quite sure."

Sitting in the nearest chair, I said, "Pandora, I'm terribly sorry."

"I knew you would be. That's why I came here. You see, the worst part is I don't know how to face people. I've known since Saturday that he wasn't coming home and I haven't told anyone. I haven't even been to work."

"How did you find out?"

"I picked the mail up after dropping Clare the other day. There was a letter from Kim. He said he'd decided to stay in Ireland — presumably for good — and then he went on for two pages with a list of the things he wanted me to pack and send."

In the silence that followed something crashed into the window behind me. I turned in time to see a bird which had stunned itself against the glass, whirr up from the ground and vanish into the mulberry tree. Turning back to Pandora, I saw she hadn't even noticed.

I went to her then, and kneeling in front of her put my hands over hers. "Perhaps it isn't . . . "

She didn't let me finish, "Yes, it is. I know it is because this is the way Kim does things. He's sneaky like a little boy. I've always known that and I didn't mind. I accepted it as being part of him and now it's worked against me. He's been so damned careful not to give me an inkling of what he meant to do. He knew that if he did, I'd be strong enough to stop him. But he's been planning it for ages. In the letter he told me he'd put in his resignation at school halfway through last term. So he's known all along and that means other people knew as well."

"Did he give you a reason when he wrote?"

"No, none at all." Pandora disengaged her hands from mine and clenched one above each breast. "I don't know if he's landed some job in Dublin or vanished into a monastery taking his recipes for wine with him."

Sitting back on my heels, I said, "Have you tried to ring him?"

"Yes, I did that on Sunday when the first shock had worn off. I rang the hotel where he'd been staying, but apparently he'd anticipated that and checked out."

"Pandora, if the worst comes to the worst and Kim doesn't come home, what will you do?"

Instead of answering the question, she said, "I worked so hard for him. He was still at uni when we met, you know. I was teaching by then and I helped put him through. After we married, I put aside the things I liked — the piano, drama, even my painting and I helped Kim instead." She stopped talking and was lost somewhere in the past. Then, focusing on me again, she said, "You asked what I'd do and I can only say I don't know. I don't know how I'll fill the gap. From the day we met I made Kim my life and obviously that is the kind of mistake you pay dearly for."

Behind me the bird thudded into the window again. When it did, Pandora put her head down on her knees and began to cry with big breathy sobs.

Kim Hunt didn't come back. The reason was simple enough — he'd fallen in love with an Irish student of oenology and decided to spend his life with her. It was to be some time before that piece of news sifted back to the Maryston Valley but all along I think, in the bottom of her heart, Pandora knew another woman was involved. Instead of sending Kim the books and papers he'd asked for, she sent everything he owned including the telescope and his English bike. God knows what it cost her in money, let alone grief, but she hired an odd-job man to crate the things and she stood over him while he did it, telling him how to pack them and later when the crates were lidded, how to drive the nails. After that Pandora threw herself into furious house cleaning as if to scour the memory of her husband out of the place, and by the time it was finished, having obtained leave of absence from her teaching job, she shut the door behind her and went to Europe for six months.

While Pandora was away, Clare and I each received a letter from her every week. They were in small curled feminine writing, the ones to me about food and continental methods of cooking, the ones to Clare about the ballet. I think Pandora saw a performance of every fair-sized ballet company in Europe and somehow managed to visit several of the schools as well. It was as if she'd decided to research a thesis on the subject and on the rare occasions when I wondered why she'd chosen dancing, I told myself that in the first place the choice had probably been accidental, but once started the ballet-hunt had become a substitute for the interest she'd taken in Kim and his thesis on Gaelic poetry and politics.

Although the letters to Clare were full of administrative detail which would have bored another girl, my daughter read them until she knew them by heart. As for the programmes and photographs Pandora sent, they were more valuable to Clare than baskets of pearls.

By then it was obvious that Clare was aiming for a career as a dancer and because I knew it was a field with few stars in it, I warned her when I got the chance about the frustrations of the corps de ballet and warned her too about the hard work, the dieting and the arthritis which turns up sooner or later. Clare's answer was to practise more determinedly than ever but I must admit that in the period while Pandora's letters were arriving regularly, Clare and I got on better than we'd done for months, and although I knew it was mainly due to the fact that Clare needed someone to share them with, I took it as a sign that gradually the difficulties in our relationship would iron themselves out.

Pandora was home for Christmas and she came to the Christmas-night dinner I had for Hannibal, Nicky Carr and old Birdie Dadswell. (Hannibal's sweetheart, Alan, was away rallying somewhere in north Africa.) Pandora had put on a lot of weight and was dressed in a short tentlike garment of black and green stripes. With it, she had on black shoes and stockings and a black toque which she left on all the evening. I don't know if the clothes were meant to be widow's weeds or the latest in Parisian chic, but I found them an extraordinary choice for the Maryston Valley on a hot summer's night.

Throughout the meal Pandora talked incessantly and her hands fluttered above her plate, reminding me again of excited birds. Mostly she talked about ballet and what she had to say bored everyone but Clare, who looked at her as if she were Cranko and Balanchine rolled into one. Whenever she stopped for a moment and there seemed some hope of changing the subject, Nicky Carr set her off again with arch questions about male ballet dancers.

The evening was saved by the arrival of Mike Duffield at the door with two bottles of imported champagne.

Duffield was fortyish with thick curly hair, an untroubled brow and Irish-looking eyes of slate-blue. He was a man who liked wearing well-cut moleskins and Harris tweed but that night he'd been at some formal function and wore a dinner jacket and black tie. I should have been surprised to see him at my place, but somehow I was not. We'd met for the first time the week before when my car ran out of petrol in front of the lush paddocks of his farm. He'd filled the tank for me, refused payment and with a grin told me to let him know if my old car got me safely home. I didn't of course, and I don't suppose I would have greeted him as effusively as I did that night if Pandora's conversation hadn't swamped my little party. As it was, I did the long-lost bit and invited him inside.

It was funny to see how the females there began to sparkle in Duffield's presence. Sitting in an armchair by the table, he stretched his legs in front of him and, as men do, took over the conversation. He flirted with Hannibal and Birdie too but paid little attention to me. I wasn't taken in by that and more than once caught him examining the room and its decorations in the manner of someone anxious to learn whatever possible about the occupant.

Hannibal put on a record of Chopin piano pieces and Clare and I, both champagne-lit, danced our version of mazurkas until red-faced and out of breath we collapsed together on the couch. Duffield watched us with a bland face and on Pandora's I thought I saw the look of hunger I'd seen there once before.

At eleven thirty, Birdie was ready for home. Duffield offered to drive her and after kisses on the cheek all round, they left. From then on, Duffield called on me once or twice a week and Hannibal, assuming we were lovers, told me my running out of petrol in front of his farm was the modern equivalent of dropping one's hankie.

"It's not like that, silly," I said. "As the movie stars say, we're just friends."

"No one believes *them* either."

"Well you can believe me. Duffield merely calls in for a chat. He talks away about his farm and income tax and stuff like that then he choofs off. In fact since I met him he hasn't made one move that could be construed as a pass."

"He doesn't need to, does he? He knows that all he has to do is wait and the day will come when you'll fall into his arms like a sun-loosened apricot."

I laughed at that and said, "Don't be mad," then added, "Anyway, don't you like him?"

"Of course I do. I think he's just what the doctor ordered."

"Meaning?"

Hannibal was mending her gym shoe with Elastoplast at the time and instead of answering she rolled her eyes at me. They were shining with amusement. Then, working again on her shoe she began to whistle. She whistled the old song "Love in Bloom" and she was still whistling when I left the room.

8

Duffield went on calling on me and so did Pandora who always seemed to be at our place either picking Clare up or dropping her off. Usually she stayed for coffee or a meal and to be fair to her I was glad of the company. Her style of dress was still outlandish. Indeed there were times when she looked as if she'd delved into her grandmother's trunk and put on something she'd found there. With the advent of winter, she began appearing in velvet cloaks trimmed with bits of fur, and turn-of-the-century hats which caused a certain amount of merriment among the locals, though Pandora didn't notice, or if she did, didn't care.

She'd joined an organisation called The Theatre Bus and with a group of other reasonably well-off women travelled to Melbourne once a month to attend a play or concert. They left Maryston by bus late in the afternoon and took their dinner with them. According to Birdie Dadswell, whose niece was one of the travellers, a lot of rivalry went on over the thermos'd meals with some of the theatregoers taking elaborate ones which included wine and after-dinner mints.

In July they went to see a performance of *Giselle* by the London Festival Ballet and when Pandora asked if Clare could go, I agreed knowing that at her age I'd have stowed away to see such stars as Nureyev and Terabust. I remember, though, being surprised that I hadn't been included in the invitation.

Clare, who'd seen live ballet only twice before, came home from Melbourne trembling to inner music, an inner dance. She was too happy to be standoffish and in the days that followed helped in the house and even made bits of conversation. I was so delighted by the change in her that I started doing corny things like chanting pieces of nonsense verse as I drove to work, and stopping in the supermarket to beam at fat country girls with fat babies.

The period of domestic chumminess lasted about a month and then Pandora asked Clare to go to Sydney with her for a week of ballet. Clare told me of the invitation when I got home from work. I'd had a tiresome day, had quarrelled with my favourite client, a good-looking Italian vegetable farmer with a boisterous laugh. On learning what his year's tax liability would be, he'd sworn at me and stormed from the office. That set the pattern and other unpleasant interviews followed. Just before closing time the day was sweetened a little by the Italian's coming back and handing me a carton of vegetables with a bunch of fresh herbs on top.

It was cold outside. I drove home as fast as I could beneath a sky of yellowish cloud. The house was cold too and the first thing I did after dumping the carton of vegetables on a chair, was kneel to light the sitting-room fire. Wind, gusting down the chimney, blew out the first two matches. Cursing, I lit a third and with that one the fire caught.

From behind me, Clare's voice said, "Mum, Pandora's got tickets for a week of ballet. It's in Sydney and she's asked me to go with her."

As she spoke, a gust of wind stronger than the others

blew smoke over me. With smarting eyes, I scrambled to my feet.

"Mum — did you hear me?" said Clare. "Pandora's got tickets for a week of ballet."

I turned to look at her. The room was growing dark but Clare, between the door and window, was caught in the last wash of daylight. My eyes, still smarting, took in the fact that she wore nothing but her school blouse and a pair of underpants. That done, they admired the red silk braid of her hair and the milk-pearl of her legs. Then, with some of the day's anxieties still nagging at me, I took time to ask myself how those fragile legs would carry her through a dancing career, let alone the mundane tasks and griefs which make up a woman's lot.

"Mother, you're not listening to me."

My voice soft, I said, "Yes, I am. I heard every word. There's a season of ballet in Sydney and you want to go."

"Yes, I do."

"And when is this momentous event? In the next school holidays?"

"No, it's now — or almost. It starts on Monday week. Pandora wants to drive, so we'd have to leave early on the Sunday."

"That's in the middle of term. You've got it wrong somehow."

"I haven't got it wrong. I've seen the tickets."

Crossing the room to switch on the light, I said, "Pandora couldn't get away in term time, so run along and put some clothes on before you catch your death." For the first time in my life I heard my mother's voice in mine.

Clare, who'd blinked once or twice as the light went on, widened her eyes and said, "Yes she can. She's got miles of sick leave saved up and she's taking some of that."

"Well she may be but she's not taking you."

At that point, the fire shot a spark into the middle of the room. We both rushed to pick it up and Clare, beating me to it, grabbed it and threw it onto the hearth. Then she faced me and with the smell of scorched wool around us, said, "Tell me why I can't go."

Poking with my toe at the burn on the rug, I said, "Calm down a little and we'll talk about it later."

She took a step towards me, her hands clasped on her chest. "I shan't calm down until you say I can go."

The childish answer made me feel a flick of exasperation. Squashing it down I said, "Look — if it's in the holidays, I promise I'll think about it."

"It's not in the holidays, I've already told you that. Why are you so thick?"

We stared at each other and I said, "I'm thick, Clare, because I don't seem to be in possession of all the facts." My voice was flat and angry.

"I've told you — Pandora . . . "

I interrupted her, "Yes, but there seems to be a piece of information missing. Pandora knows damned well I wouldn't let you go haring off somewhere while school's on."

"Pandora said school doesn't matter, that I wouldn't miss anything of consequence. Anyway she said she'll give me extra lessons when we get back so I'll catch up."

"Pandora should mind her own business."

"I *am* her business. She told me so. She told me I'm as much her daughter as yours. That someday all the things she has will be mine and she said that on the day I dance as a professional, she'll give me the ring with the freshwater pearl in it."

"If Pandora said all of that, she's very naughty." I used the nursery word deliberately. "Now go to your room and put some clothes on."

91

Not moving, Clare said, "You're not going to let me go, are you?"

"Indeed I'm not."

She was watching my face. "Are you going to stop me seeing Pandora?"

"No, why should I?"

"She said you might."

"That was naughty of her too."

Still watching me, Clare changed tack. "Vinnie, I really want to go."

"Yes, I know you do."

"Then let me."

"Not this time."

"Why not? Tell me that."

I heard myself sigh. "The reason won't seem a good one to you, but I want you to learn, now, before you get any older that life never lets us snatch bonbons for nothing. There's always a price and because of that it's better to make the payment first."

"That's not a reason. It's waffle."

"Then I'll give you another one. It's in no way suitable for you to go under the circumstances you've put forward. As your mother, I've made that decision and I'll stick to it."

Clare was no longer looking at me. She was looking at the floor. I couldn't see her expression, but guessing she knew she'd lost the battle and was close to tears, I said, "Pandora had no right to proffer the invitation, but that wasn't your fault and to stop your heart breaking, I'll take you to Melbourne the next time there's some ballet on."

Getting no reply, I went on, "I doubt the car would get us that far but we can go on the train. We can go for the whole weekend and see two performances."

Clare raised her eyes. I'd been wrong about the tears,

there were none. Instead, her eyes were full of temper. "I'll get Pandora to ring you," she said and made for the door.

With temper of my own, I called after her, "That won't be necessary. I intend to ring the lady myself the minute I've had my dinner."

As it happened, Pandora beat me to it. Halfway through the meal she rang to ask if Clare had told me the news. The self-confidence in her voice fanned my anger. "What news was that?" I asked.

"About Sydney. I want to take her to the ballet."

"Oh, yes — she told me and we disposed of that an hour ago."

There was silence from Pandora, then she said, "I take it you don't approve."

"I certainly don't and although I realise you meant to be kind, I think it'd be better in future if you put things to me first. As it is, Clare's been hurt for nothing."

"But Vinnie, surely her career . . . "

She got no further because my voice came in over hers, "For Christ's sake, Pandora, what career? She's thirteen years old! At that age I thought the entire world was going to wait outside the stage door for me. With Clare, anything could happen, so give her time to be a child a little longer."

"Give her time you mean to fall in love with some dairy farmer's son and ruin her life."

"Yes, exactly, if that's what she wants to do."

"I think you'll find that Clare has other ideas."

"Then what are we talking about?"

After another silence, Pandora, with almost a singing note in her voice said, "I can see you're too upset to be rational, so we'll let the matter drop, shall we?" And without another word, she rang off.

Clare didn't mention the Sydney trip to me again, indeed she mentioned nothing. She'd sent me back to Coventry and only answered when I forced her to. I was less prepared this time though to put up with her silence. Feeling I'd done little to deserve it, I let her know more than once that she was being rude. In spite of that, the silence was maintained for almost a week, then one morning as I was hurrying to get some breakfast onto the table, Clare appeared in the hall. Dressed for school and standing just outside the kitchen door, she said, "Would you mind not talking to the animals. I can't bear listening to it."

With the skin of a half-squeezed orange in my hand, I stood and gaped at her. I don't think she felt too sure of her ground at that moment because she hesitated before saying, "You talk to them all the time. I hear your voice go on and on and I can't think."

Still not moving, I said, "Have you gone mad or something?"

That triggered some defiance in Clare. "If you must know," she said, "I've wanted to tell you for a long time but didn't know how."

"Not to talk to the dog and cat?"

"Yes."

I went to the sink, put the orange skin down and with my back to Clare, said, "Talking to the animals is part of my life — part of theirs too."

"Well I can't stand it. I try to blot out your voice by putting my hands over my ears but I can still hear it. I even hear it in my room."

I'd turned by then and was facing her. "I've no one else to talk to, Clare," I said. "Is that what you want from me? No one to talk to, not even a bloody dog or cat?"

I must have looked pretty wild because Clare took a

step backwards and for a moment seemed to crouch against the wall. Beside her was the Chinese tapestry where I'd killed the huntsman spider and cried for the first time for Brook. From there Clare gave me a look which was a mixture of fright, defiance and something else I couldn't read. Then she straightened up and hurried to her room. In a little while the back door slammed and I knew she'd gone to school without any food.

I spent a miserable day at work, not doing much and what I did, I did mechanically. Most of the time, I thought about my daughter. It was no longer possible to fool myself that she was suffering the kind of grief and growing pains that time would heal. There was something else, some kind of deep-seated trouble between us and to find out what it was, I needed help. When I'd worked that out, I rang my doctor's surgery and made an appointment to see him that evening. In the past when I'd taken troubles to him, he'd laughed at me and made me laugh too. That was fair enough; most of my troubles *had* been laughable. This trouble was not and I believed he'd hear me out and then agree to refer me to a psychologist or some sort of family counsellor.

The appointment with my doctor was never kept. When I got home from work, although there were lights in the house, no sounds of *Swan Lake* were emanating from Clare's room. Still in my coat, I went to see what she was doing, and more to the point, if she would talk to me.

She was in her room. Standing with her back to the door, she was packing clothes into our one good suitcase which lay open on the bed with little piles of underclothes and things beside it.

Stupidly, I said, "What are you doing?"

Not turning, she said, "That's obvious, isn't it?"

"All right — I'll start again. Why are you packing?"

Clare took her dressing-gown from the end of the bed, folded it and put it in the case. When that was done, she said, "I'm going to live with Pandora. She's coming for me at six."

I was too surprised to speak, just stood in the doorway with my bag still on my shoulder and a funny feeling in my throat.

Clare moved her head enough to shoot a glance at me. "I hope you're not going to carry on," she said.

Finally, I found my voice. "You can't be serious."

Picking up another pile of clothes, Clare said, "Yes I am. Pandora and I have talked about it a lot."

"Then Pandora should have more sense. You aren't old enough to leave home. You don't have my permission."

She swung around then and with eyes that seemed darker than usual, looked at me. "You'd have to go to court," she said, "to stop me."

I couldn't read the expression on her face. It was the one I'd seen that morning in the hall, the mixture of defiance and fright and something else I couldn't recognise. In any case, I should have gone to her and put my arms around her and said, "My beautiful child, we've made a mess of things. Let's start again." But I didn't. All I did was say, "Would you let me do that? Would you let me go to court?"

Watching me, she whispered, "Yes."

"Then you'd better go," I said and turned away.

I don't know what I did for the next half hour. I think I took my coat off and fed the animals. I'm not sure. I think too that once I went back to Clare's room to ask if we could talk things over and she said, "There's no point."

I got myself a drink, I know that because I was standing with it in my hand, looking out onto the bare orchard, when Pandora came into the room behind me.

"I hope you won't feel badly about this, Vinnie," was what she had the gall to say. "I'm sure it's for the best."

Slowly I turned and looked at her. She was wearing a big brown cloak and had some sort of turban on her head. I didn't speak and she went on, "This way you can be free to get on with your life." And she gave me what I can only describe as an arch look. "Clare and I can devote ourselves to the ballet. She'll be a star one day and you'll be proud of her."

I wanted to go to her and mark her fat smooth face with my hands and I remember wondering if I was going mad. She must have had the same thought because she backed towards the door.

"Are you taking the cat?" I said. "It's Clare's you know. But if you do, I advise you not to speak to it."

She had no idea what I was talking about but after opening and closing her mouth, she opened it again to say, "I've already realised that Clare will miss her animals and I've ordered her a Burmese cat from Nance Durbin."

Not raising my voice, I burnt my bridges by saying, "You bitch — you cunning bitch."

Her neck and then her face went red and while I watched the face seemed to blow up in size. We glared at each other, then without another word, she turned and rushed towards Clare's room. After a little while, I heard her car drive away and when I went to look in the bedroom it was empty. My daughter had gone too.

9

In the days that followed Clare's departure, my mind was like a switchboard that had jammed. It simply wouldn't work. Which is another way of saying I really had gone mad. Hannibal was frantic about me. "Do something," she said. "Go to the police." But I did nothing. I didn't even go to work. Instead I crouched at home listening all the time for the telephone, listening too for the hiss of car tyres out on the road.

When Hannibal had told me to go to the police, I'd laughed a mad laugh and said, "What for? My daughter won't stay with that woman. She'll come home, you'll see." I kept that up for three days and three dry-eyed nights, while Clare didn't even telephone, let alone come home. Then, because Hannibal looked at me too kindly when putting a cup of coffee in front of me, I began to cry.

"What *are* you going to do?" asked Hannibal.

"Nothing," I said, as soon as I could speak. "I'm going to sit tight — make no effort and in the end, Clare will come back to me."

Astounded, Hannibal was searching for an argument to use, when I said, "Last night I asked Brook what to do and he answered me. 'Go on loving her,' he said, 'that's all you have to do'."

The look on Hannibal's face made me rush to add,

"All right — perhaps I *did* imagine it, but you know as well as I do that to Brook, loving meant letting go. He used to say that the only way to keep something, was to let it go. So that's what I'll do. I'll let Clare go until she's ready to come back, and I'll find other ways to show my love as well."

"That sort of thing might have been all right for Brook," said Hannibal, "but not for you."

She was right. My resolve lasted one more day then after dark it left me. With fingers which shook and fumbled, I rang Pandora's number and asked to speak to Clare.

Sounding smug, Pandora told me that Clare was out with friends, playing tennis.

Clare playing tennis? In the dark? My daughter who scorned all sport and wouldn't know how to hold a racquet much less wield one.

Certain Pandora was lying, what could I do but hang up without hearing any more? Later though, I heard a car, heard it stop outside my gate and with my heart going like a hammer, I flew to the door. It wasn't Clare who came in, it was Duffield and when I saw his wide accommodating chest in front of me, I put my face against it. That was the night of course, I fell into Duffield's arms as Hannibal had predicted. But I wasn't any sun-loosened apricot, I was a pale lost moon falling from the sky.

Duffield wasn't the greatest lover in the world nor the most imaginative. He was a comfortable and friendly lover and maybe that's the best of all. Anyway it was marvellous to lie with him in my old soft bed and for a little while be someone who felt cherished. I must admit that the pleasure sex gave me at that time was surprisingly sharp. I was glad of that and in no way ashamed because it taught me that in spite of everything Vinnie Beaumont

99

had her own identity and that life did indeed go on.

Surprisingly, Duffield was inclined to see merit in my passive attitude to Clare's absence. Hannibal said that was because he didn't particularly want my daughter home again. Whatever the reason, the support he gave me kept me going for almost three weeks and even now I believe that if I'd had the nerve to stick it out, I might have won.

As it was, I sent Clare little notes — one or two a week — just flimsy things with news of the garden and the animals. I was careful not to take a mournful tone, even more careful not to take an accusing one. Trying to strike the balance between lightness and concern, I rewrote most of the notes more than once and for all of that, I didn't get a single answer. I sent money too, a cheque each Friday made out to Pandora for a little more than I estimated Clare's keep to be. Those cheques were a gamble on my part. When I sent the first one, I half expected it to be returned. On the other hand, I believed that underneath her apparent generosity, Pandora was an avaricious woman who'd be unable to resist money once she'd fingered it. And I was right because although Pandora didn't once acknowledge receipt, each cheque was presented at my bank the Tuesday after I'd posted it.

There were times of course during the weeks in question when my courage wobbled, times when I wanted to rush to Pandora's house and order my daughter home. And there were other times when I'd remember Clare's narrow little shoulders and worry that Pandora was too concerned with fine food and the arts to find time to air the sheets properly.

Once at lunchtime I went to the high school and peered through the gate like some dimwitted female Humbert Humbert. I didn't catch a glimpse of Clare and perhaps it was just as well. In the end, the thing that brought me to my knees was nothing more dramatic than the sight of two schoolboys hopping off the bus outside my office. The bus was held up in traffic and the boys got off and went up the street squabbling like a pair of sparrows. For some reason that little sequence was more than I could bear and the next minute with my hands fumbling again, I rang Duffield to say, "I can't bear it any longer. I want to talk to a solicitor."

He didn't argue, just said he'd make me an appointment with Con Smythe for the next day.

I knew Smythe well enough by sight though I hadn't met him. He had clever, slightly goitrous eyes and an elegant little moustache. Known as one of Maryston's Galahads, he wore pure wool suits of powder blue and ties which picked up the blue exactly. Altogether he was the last man I'd have taken my troubles to but when I said as much to Duffield, he pushed aside my doubts by saying, "Nonsense. He's a bloody good solicitor and he'll look after you — he's a mate of mine."

The air in Con Smythe's office smelt faintly of cigar smoke and the carpet was rich and dark. As for the man himself, he greeted me with charm and a soft voice, but I can tell you it was no fun sitting opposite him spilling my story while he wrote down everything I said.

At the end of it, he looked up. "And you want your daughter back, of course." His voice was so quiet, I had to lean forward to hear him.

I said, "Yes," and when he didn't respond, blurted, "I'll get her, won't I?"

"You shouldn't have much difficulty. Mrs Hunt has no legal right to her. There are a couple of things though that might be awkward if she decides to fight. You say that Clare went willingly?"

"Yes."

"And you let her go?"

"I was hurt and angry. Anyone would have been."

"Quite." Smythe studied his notes. "And you've sent a cheque for her maintenance each week?"

"Yes."

"Starting when?"

"The first week."

He looked up again. "Why did you do that?"

"To show that she was mine, that's all."

Smythe didn't comment on my reply and I said, "Was that a mistake?"

"Not necessarily." He mumbled something I didn't catch, then, "But you haven't been to Mrs Hunt's house or made any attempt to get Clare back?"

"No."

"Why not?"

"Because I thought she'd come back herself. The quarrel was over nothing really. My mother and I had a hundred such fights but in the end each one was forgiven and forgotten. I thought it would be the same with Clare — that she'd sulk for a few days and then be glad to come home."

Smythe leaned back in his chair, and watching me, stroked one side of his moustache with his pen. Then he said, "As I see it, Vinnie — may I call you that?"

I nodded.

"As I see it, the thing to do at this stage is negotiate with Mrs Hunt. You've nothing to lose by doing that and everything to gain."

"If she has no right to Clare, why should I negotiate?"

"Because for everyone's sake, I think you'd be wise to avoid a court case."

With a thread of panic in my voice, I said, "Why do you say that?"

"In the first place, there's the matter of your relationship with Duff. It is, I suppose . . . " he paused.

102

I made myself meet his eyes, "I'm sure it's exactly what you think."

"That would come out in court, you know." Smythe cleared his throat. "Along with anything else of a scandalous nature that Mrs Hunt can ferret out."

Still meeting his eyes, I said, "She'd find a few things. I've not been what you'd call discreet but surely that wouldn't cost me my daughter."

"No, I don't think it would but we have to take into account the damage it might do in other directions."

I thought that over, "You mean Duffield and his marriage?"

"That's one consideration."

In the silence that followed someone in the next room let go with a machine-gun burst on the typewriter. The sound stopped then started again and I said, "I've no wish to make things difficult for Duffield. In fact that's the last thing I want."

"I thought you'd feel that way."

"So there's nothing I can do?"

"Come on now, things aren't as black as that. In the first place Mrs Hunt doesn't know you won't go to court. That's where your bargaining power comes in. If you have things you'd rather hide, you can be sure she has too."

I was looking at the floor when I heard him say, "Could there be anything, well, unnatural about Mrs Hunt's regard for Clare?"

Raising my eyes to his, I said, "Do you mean is she a lesbian?"

"To put it bluntly, yes."

"I must admit the thought has crossed my mind, but I'm sure she's not. She's broody, that's all, and she's taken my child to replace the one who got away to Ireland."

Smythe was amused and let it show. "No doubt you're right," he said. "Look — why don't you let me get in touch with her; I know her slightly. I can tell her you're contemplating legal action and see what the response is."

With the typewriter still firing next door I thought for a while then nodded my head, "I guess there's nothing else for me to do," and drained by the interview I said goodbye and left.

Not having heard from Con Smythe by the end of the next week, I rang his office to be told he was at a conference in Sydney. I rang every day the following week but it was Friday before I saw him. Then, instead of sending for me, he came to my office, where he skirted my jungle of pot plants, smoothed his hand over his hair and said something which was lost in the sound of semi-trailer gears being changed out in the street.

"Hell," he said when the semi had passed, "how do you work in this din?"

"A lot of the time I don't." I'd stood up mechanically and answered the same way while my eyes searched his face for news of Clare.

"May I sit?" He waited with his hand on the back of the chair.

"Of course — I'm sorry." We both sat.

"I've news for you." Con smiled at me. "I've talked to Mrs Hunt."

I didn't answer, just slid my hands below the level of the desk and waited.

"She sailed into my rooms ready I'm sure to tell me how to run my practice, but she lost a lot of her wind when I told you you were prepared to go to court."

Leaning forward, I said, "Go on."

"It was extraordinary really. She paused just long enough to get a cigarette alight, then put forward a plan for reconciliation. One can't help thinking the whole thing's been an almighty bluff."

"Then she's giving Clare back?"

"Well at the moment she's not going that far, but she's come up with a scheme which is probably just as good."

Again I waited.

"Apparently she's pulled a lot of strings and got Clare an audition for next month at the Victorian College of the Arts. If she's accepted as a pupil, she'd start there in the new year, but the thing is, of course, none of it's possible without your signature on the application form."

"The woman's mad. As if I'd agree."

Before answering, Con picked up my paperweight, a starfish made of glass. Turning it over in his hand, he said, "The idea may be worth considering."

"I wouldn't dream of letting her go."

"I can't see why not. She'd be leaving Mrs Hunt and going to live in Melbourne instead."

"But Pandora would go too. That's why she's suggested it."

Con put the starfish back on the desk. "Then make it a condition of your agreement that you choose the place where Clare lives."

"She'd have to board and she's too young for that."

"She's doing it already."

"But Melbourne! God, she's only thirteen."

"Mrs Hunt says she's very keen to go."

"Of course she is. She sees only the glamorous side of it." I brought my elbows forward and planted them on the desk. "Look, I'd planned that if Clare still wanted to study ballet when she'd done year ten here at High, I'd try to get her into the Australian Ballet School. She'd be almost sixteen then."

"Don't overlook the point, though, that she may not

105

be accepted now and in the meantime you can make it another condition of your approval that Clare comes home to you at once."

"Pandora wouldn't fall for that."

"I think she might. Although she did her best not to show it, she was rattled by the mention of a court case. She could lose her job over something like this, and I'm sure she's smart enough to know it."

"Then I should just demand Clare back and stick to my original plan."

"But in disappointing Clare, you could strengthen her regard for Mrs Hunt."

We were both silent while another truck ground by and then I said, "What would *you* do?"

Con told me it wasn't his place to make a decision for me then went on immediately to say, "My advice is to agree to Mrs Hunt's plan and take a gamble on Clare's failing the audition. That way you win on all counts. And even if she doesn't fail, I'd say that you'd come out of it pretty well."

Another silence, a longer one. In the end I broke it to say, "I guess you're right. I guess it's the sensible thing to do, but only, mind you, if my terms are met."

"They will be," he said. "You'll see."

Con was right. After several days of phone calls and prevarication, Pandora gave in and on Wednesday afternoon, I left work early and, picking up Billie on the way, went to collect my daughter.

No one was in sight at Pandora's but Clare's suitcase had been carried to the top of the steps and left beside a clump of blackberries, where it looked abandoned and as sad as hell. The first thing I did when I pulled up was grab it and put it in the boot of the car.

The day was the first warm one we'd had that spring and in the north thunderclouds were marshalling. The

106

little valley beyond Pandora's garden was full of blue shadows and newly budded willow trees. I didn't look at them, instead I looked at the house. All the windows were shut and all the drapes were drawn.

I was halfway down the steps when one of the windows slid open and Clare came out. She was carrying a pile of books with a pair of shoes balanced on top. Behind her the window slid shut again.

Without looking at me, Clare walked to the steps and began to climb. I suppose it was my imagination but she seemed taller and thinner than she'd been when she left home. Two steps below me, she dropped one of the shoes and as she stooped to pick it up, the other fell too. I went down to help her and as I picked up a shoe, she said, "Thanks, Mum," but her hair hid her face and I had no idea what she was thinking.

Upright again, I took most of the books away from her and when I did, she bounded up the remaining steps and flew to the car for a boisterous reunion with Billie.

So we went home but somewhere between seeing Clare's suitcase sitting by the blackberries and seeing the window of the house slide shut behind her, a change had taken place in me and I could think of nothing to say. It wasn't as if I tried out bits of conversation in my mind and discarded them, I simply thought of nothing. We drove in silence and in a little while I stole a look at Clare. She'd wound the window down and with her face turned away from me was holding her hair up off her neck so what breeze there was would reach her skin. From the little I could see of her she was untouched and unmoved by the battle which had raged around her. I thought then of the woman we'd left to mourn behind her drawn curtains like a fat dove someone had blinded, and for the life of me I couldn't understand why I hadn't gone to her in the preceding weeks and tried to reach some kind of compromise.

107

We went on, past paddocks faintly washed with green, past orchard rows starred here and there with the first spring blossom. Lightning began to flicker in the sky and still I found nothing to say.

At Gorrangher, just before we reached the road where we lived, I finally spoke. "It's okay, you know, if you see Pandora now and then."

Clare didn't answer and I said, "Would you like that?"

Turning her head, she said, "Sure, that's fine," and they were the only words we said to each other between Pandora's place and our front gate.

The rest is easy enough to tell. Clare auditioned at the college and was accepted as a student for the coming year. Although she and I were together a lot in making the arrangements for the move, we didn't manage to renew the relationship which had bound us so sweetly when she was little. Instead we spent the time in being unnecessarily polite to each other and filling in the silences with inconsequentials.

Mrs Curno helped us find a place for her to board and at the end of January when she left to live in South Melbourne, I think it was a relief to both of us.

I don't know if she was homesick for Maryston. Certainly she showed no sign of it. At the college, her marks for school work were above average, and for dance and mime they were excellent.

During the first year she came home for all the holidays and twice a month I visited her in Melbourne. We'd go to lunch and then to a movie or some such thing, but we were finding less and less to talk about and at the end of the day, I'd catch the train home, saddened by the knowledge that we were never likely to be friends.

The next year she found a friend at the college, a dark-haired dimpled giggler called Emma Nesbitt.

Although as different as chalk and cheese, the two girls were mad about each other and Clare took to spending most of her holidays on the Nesbitt farm at Bacchus Marsh. In the little I saw of Emma, she went out of her way to be pleasant to me. For my part, I was delighted to see Clare participating in a normal teenage relationship and encouraged it as much as I could.

Ironically, although I hardly saw Clare in those days, I began to see a little of Pandora Hunt. She'd sold her house and moved into Maryston where she threw herself into revitalising the Art Appreciation Society and later the Historical Society as well. Like ageing beauties who'd been discarded by the same man, we took comfort now and then in telephone conversations about Clare's life away from us, and once, in the company of Mrs Curno, journeyed to Melbourne together to a Christmas break-up at the college.

Clare danced that night. She danced first with five other girls then alone for about a minute and a half. On the way back to Maryston, when Pandora and Mrs Curno grew eloquent on the subject of her grace and technique, I held my tongue for it seemed to me there was missing from her dancing the quality of fire or poetry or whatever it is that Art demands from its favourites.

The following August, Irene died and soon after that Duffield came to tell me he'd decided to buy a South Australian property famous for its gracious buildings and classy horses. Leaning against the piano, he blew a cloud of smoke into the air and said, "We plan to live in Adelaide a lot of the year. That way the girls can go to a decent school."

He'd made no mention of his marriage but watching him I sensed that in my absence it had reached and survived some crisis point. Not only that — Duffield was glad that it had.

109

"Perhaps you'll get over to South Australia now and then," he said.

"You know damned well I won't." My let's-have-no-bullshit tone made Duffield laugh. I laughed too and after that our parting took place in an atmosphere of matey good spirits. It was, I think, a fitting way for our affair to end.

The next to leave my little circle was Hannibal, who came into my garden one citrus-scented evening in October to tell me she was going overseas with Alan Weston. Keeping her eyes on Birdie Dadswell's cow as it ate grass through the fence, she said, "Alan's signed a contract to drive in Europe and it may be several years before we come back."

Dumb with shock, I heard her sweet Nina Simone voice say, "We're getting married before we go and I'd like it to be here."

What could I do but push my dismay out of sight behind a cheerful face?

Years before, Hannibal had declared that when she married, she'd do it in what she called the Zorba style, dispensing with such things as churches and civil celebrants. It turned out that she'd meant what she said. In the company of a few friends, she and Alan stood together in my orchard and pronounced themselves married, while bees with pollen-laden legs droned by and a pilot friend of Alan's wrote "Good Roads to the Bride and Groom" in the sky overhead.

Late at night when everyone had gone, I wandered through the house then went to sit on the step where I used to sit with Beauregard. There, in a post-wedding, post-champagne depression, I realised that the part of my life which could be labelled youth had ended. It was then that I decided to accept my brother's offer and go back to Queensland.

The only other thing I have to tell about that period is that through all of it I went on writing Clare the flimsy little notes I'd started when she ran away to Pandora. I wrote one or two a week, sometimes only half a page with whatever news I had. The first year she answered a few of them, then she stopped, ringing me instead when she wanted something. I went on writing them, though, even when I felt she didn't bother to read them. And when I'd finally packed and moved, I still sent them, one or two a week. But I didn't tell anyone about them; I didn't even tell that I had a daughter, because I knew that if I did, I'd find it too hard explaining why she didn't answer any of those silly little notes.

THE
ESTUARY

10

A man was leaning against the fence of the Catholic church. His eyes were shut and he was whistling. Inside, someone was getting married. The organist was letting fly with "Ave Maria" and the man outside was whistling it. He was whistling so loudly the people in the church must have been able to hear him and he was whistling so melodiously some of them probably had panicky thoughts about where the sound was coming from.

I stopped for a moment to look at the whistler. He was somewhere between thirty-five and forty and his clothes told me that he wasn't Australian. They had a foreign cut, Russian perhaps, though I wasn't sure. As for the man himself, he had straight black hair and high cheekbones. His skin was olive with a few faint pockmarks on it.

Becoming aware of me somehow, he opened his eyes. They were long and hazel with a slight tilt at the outside corners. Fixing them on me, he said, "Gounod's 'Ave Maria' — the beginning and end of all music." Then he closed his eyes again and went back to whistling. His voice was deep and soft with a foreign rhythm in it but very little accent. I walked on hoping I'd see him again but reminding myself that many people drifted into the settlement at The Estuary and out again. Indeed there were times when I felt the entire world drifted through it at least once.

I thought about the whistler all the way to the post office but I forgot him when the woman behind the counter told me they were looking for a bookkeeper at The Bananas.

Not believing my ears, I said, "That place opposite the jetty?"

"Yes."

"The old Louisiana-looking house where they have all the parties?"

"It's a private hotel, not a house."

"God, how marvellous — I'll apply."

Scooping my letters up, Mrs Wiley said, "You mightn't get it," and when I didn't answer, "Anyway, it won't be all moonlight and roses, you know." Then leaning across the counter, she became confidential. "I can't think what books *they'd* keep. They don't sell liquor and I've heard half the guests don't pay."

"After lunch I'll go and find out," I told her.

On my way home I thought about The Bananas. Its real name was the inappropriate one of Mimosa View. Years before, some departing guests had called it The Bananas and the name had stuck. I used to pass the place in the late afternoons when I took Billie down to the beach. As I pushed my way through the Queensland heat, I'd look through the gateway with envious eyes. I'd see the half-acre slope of lawn, then steps as wide as a grandstand and the cool-looking shadows of the veranda. At that time of day a collection of people would be lolling there in cane chairs — godlike young men in surf shorts and girls in rainbow swimsuits so brief they took your breath away. Behind the sound of their talk and laughter I'd hear a marvellous tinny old jazz record being played.

To look through the gateway made me feel like an Antipodean version of the Little Match Girl. I always wanted to stay and watch but pride rather than good manners made me move on.

When I called about the job the place seemed deserted. Certainly there was no one on the veranda. That wasn't surprising. The sun was pouring death rays at it, and remembering the pensioners I saw in the general store with bandages covering their skin cancers, I pulled my hat more firmly onto my head as I started up the drive.

I was halfway to the steps when a pistol went off behind me. I jumped and spun to face the gate. No one was there. Then out of the corner of my eye I saw a movement on the lawn. Cautiously I turned my head. A man with a stockwhip in his hand was standing near a frangipanni tree. Pieces of cream petal were scattered in the grass around him. As I watched, he swung the whip around his head, swung his body too and ripped his arm downwards. Crack! I heard the pistol shot again and bits of blossom flew in the air.

After the performance the man tucked his shirt in with his free hand, then with the whip under his arm and the lash trailing, came towards me. He was smiling slightly and as he walked he watched my face. When he was within a few feet of me, he said, "I hope I didn't frighten you."

"You did a bit. It sounded like a gun."

My answer pleased him. He beamed at me, then put out his hand and said, "I'm Victor Bogle, and this is my little hotel."

While I told him who I was and what I was doing there, I took stock of him. He was about forty-five and I decided that for someone who filled in his spare moments with a stockwhip he was very nattily dressed.

117

His white linen slacks and shirt of lemon and white checks would have been just right in a Bacardi advertisement. A lock of pale hair hung over his forehead, and his eyes, brown and narrow, stared at me with surprising intensity.

As my sales talk petered out, Bogle said, "Capital. Super. Let's go inside and talk."

We went up the grandstand steps, then across the veranda and through the front door. We were in a large dark room with a billiard table and a lot of stereo equipment. Folding chairs, the kind they use in army mess halls, stood around the walls. Leading out of the room was a hall which seemed to go on forever. It too was dark but it was slashed twice by patches of light where other halls ran across it. Later, I learned that the hotel was built, or perhaps had grown, in the shape of the Cross of Lorraine.

With his hand in the small of my back, Bogle guided me towards the long hall. I smelt the smell I'd come to recognise as a Queensland one, a blend of dampness, vegetation and cats' pee.

Walking quickly, we spun into the first arm of the cross and then into an office. It was lit by sun filtered through bamboo blinds. Imagining myself working there I had a quick look around as I sat down. The room was furnished with an antique dining table and chairs One of the chairs was broken and its back lay on the table. I had time to take in two bookcases crammed with books and, hanging crookedly on the walls, some photographs of young men in what looked like university groups. Then Bogle threw his whip on the table and said, "You'll take the job of course."

"Hang on," I said, "I don't know anything about it and you don't know anything about me."

"You've told me your track record. Couldn't be better. You're just what we need."

I was about to ask him some questions when he added, "It's live-in, of course." And again I was aware of the intensity of his stare.

"I live only a mile away. I could come every day on my bike."

He answered in a voice which was suddenly lower and firmer. "No, we like the staff to live in. It's a family show and we like to keep it that way."

"I've got animals," I told him. "A dog and a cat. I couldn't leave them."

"Super. Bring them with you. The kids'll love them." Sensing, I suppose, that I was ready with more objections, he went on quickly, "We'll put you on the east side. There's a room there with a door out into the garden. You and your menagerie can settle in there and be out of everyone's way."

The idea of moving to The Bananas was tempting. Two weeks before, a colleague of Bart's had offered him an enormous sum for a six month lease on Irene's house. Bart hadn't accepted but I felt he'd wanted to.

"How many guests do you have?" I asked Bogle, "And what would my duties be?"

He dodged the question about the guests by saying, "They come and go. As I told you, we run the place as a family show. A lot of people who stay here *are* family, or as good as. And as for the duties — the usual thing — answering the phone, doing the books and so on." Bogle had been standing up but at that point he sat in the broken-backed chair and leaning forward, said, "Faith, my wife, is a teacher — a music teacher and a part-time school teacher as well. Naturally she's out a lot, and we've got twins, six-year-olds, Jami and Peta — both girls, by the way. What we need as much as anything is someone to be here with them in the afternoons." His tone was friendly, almost conspiratorial, and it was easy

119

for me to guess that we'd arrived at the nub of the matter. I guessed too that Bogle was afraid what he'd just said would put me off. He couldn't have been more wrong; the thought of having two little girls to moon over was too good to be true. For the life of me I couldn't stop myself grinning as I told Bogle I'd like to take the job.

He was delighted. Without giving me a chance to ask about pay or hours, he stood up and pushed his chair back under the table. "Super," he said, "I knew you'd take it as soon as we met. Come on, we'll have a drink to celebrate."

We went out into the hall and again with Bogle's hand at my back, we marched through the building. I thought he was taking me to a sitting room or perhaps the dining room. Instead we went to a bathroom. As Bogle opened the door, I saw an old-fashioned dentist's chair in the corner beside the bath. Suspended from the ceiling above it was a drill.

For the second time that day Bogle was enjoying my reaction. Not taking his eyes from my face, he reached towards a cupboard on the wall and shot it open. Inside were bottles with chemicals in them and two sets of partly made false teeth.

"Were you a dentist?" I asked.

"I still am. I work in here sometimes." Then, bending and shooting open a lower cupboard, he said, "It's also the bar."

I saw another row of bottles — whisky, gin, brandy, Schnapps and at least two kinds of rum.

"Don't tell me what you'll have," said Bogle, grabbing the gin bottle. "I can see you're a G and T girl." And still enjoying my surprise, he went to a fridge behind the door and took from it tonic water, a lemon and two chilled glasses.

I sat on the side of the bath to watch him mix the drinks. Handing me one, he said, "Being a private show, we're not allowed to sell grog, but we've evolved a system which works very well. As I said before, most of the people who stay here are friends. I serve them with whatever grog they want and the next day they replace it. That way we keep up the supply without contravening the licensing laws."

"Are the guests honest about it? I mean, do they put back as much as they take?"

"Some do and some don't. It evens out. There's always the idiot who drinks the cupboard dry and leaves, but someone else will be overgenerous. People who book in for dinner, of course, come on a BYO basis." Bogle was about to say more, but from somewhere in the hotel a woman's voice called his name. He stuck his head out into the hall and called back, "In here, darls." Then to me, he said, "Faith's home from class."

In a moment Faith Bogle came to the bathroom door. She was a pale woman dressed in black. She had big, heavily-lidded blue eyes and auburn hair cut in a Botticelli fan of waves. Under her arm was a shabby music case. I could tell she was tired by the way her shoulders drooped and her weight was rested on one hip. The black dress wasn't doing a thing for her but I knew that in another colour and on another day she'd be a beautiful woman.

When she saw the glass in Bogle's hand, she said, "Victor, you . . . " Then her voice tailed off as she caught sight of me.

Bogle kissed her cheek. "Vinnie Beaumont, darling," he said. "She's on the staff — our new bookkeeper."

Hardly hearing him, his wife started to speak, then realising what he'd said, she turned her blue gaze on me.

121

She gave herself time to take in my denim clothes and my canvas shoes, and when she had, she said, "Have you had any experience in this kind of work?"

"Of course she has, darling." Bogle pushed a gin and tonic into her hand. "She's had miles. She's an expert in income tax — the books here will be child's play to her." Then, giving away the fact that he'd known all along who I was, he told her I was a writer. It was something I hadn't mentioned about myself.

Faith Bogle's face lit up a bit at that piece of news. She asked me what sort of stuff I wrote but before I could answer, Bogle said, "You haven't forgotten, have you, Faithie, that a party of eight has booked in for dinner tonight?"

She was stunned. Her eyes searched his face and if anything, her own face grew paler.

"I told you last night, Faithie." As he said it, I had the feeling Bogle was enjoying himself.

"You're a swine, honestly, Victor. You didn't tell me at all." She put her drink up in the open cupboard. "I can't cope with eight tonight. I'm playing at a fashion parade in the hall at two thirty and at five I'm rehearsing *The Mikado* at the school. Somewhere in between I have to pick the children up from Stuart's and on top of that, yesterday's dishes — mountains of them — are languishing on the sink."

They stared at each other.

Reinforcing the words by pausing between them, Faith said, "There is no way I can have eight people here tonight."

From my perch on the side of the bath I said, "Can I help?"

They turned as one and as one they said, "Would you?"

So I started my job at The Bananas there and then. I

started with the dishes. That was appropriate. I soon learned there was no other full-time staff. There'd been a girl — a kid of sixteen. On Regatta Day after meeting an American with a yacht, she'd come back to the hotel, packed her clothes in a Fijian basket and sailed away. I was her replacement. A middle-aged woman called Mrs Bert, who whistled an endless repertoire of military marches through her teeth as she worked, was supposed to come in one day a week and help with the vacuuming and washing, but an invalid husband and a family of wayward children kept her home more often than not. On the days when she failed to appear, Faith and I would toss a coin to see which one of us was going to whirr the faulty vacuum cleaner around the rooms and which one was going to put the sheets and towels through the clattering old washing-machine which stood out in the garage.

In spite of the fact that I was working most of the time as a domestic and nursemaid, I'd entered into one of the happiest periods of my life. Within the boundaries of my job I had a great deal of freedom. I was free to think about my stories and to pause as often as I wished to watch the yachts that slid past the window like big butterflies. On top of that, I was part of a family again and I liked the feeling of security it gave me.

Faith seldom managed to get home to lunch and Victor usually kept out of the way during the day but the twins were always with me from half past twelve onwards. I'd give them lunch then take them to the beach for an hour. When we got home the three of us would throw ourselves, still smelling of salt and sun-screen, onto my bed. We'd pretend we were on the Star-Ship Maryston way out in space. In minutes we'd be asleep. About five when we woke the girls would go to the music room for piano lessons with their mother and I'd be free till seven or so.

My room was like a tunnel, long and narrow with a door at each end. The walls were stained and in places mouldy, but after I'd tacked up some prints and posters and tied a coloured silk scarf over the lamp it seemed to me as marvellous as any star-ship. I slept under a mosquito net and apart from anything else I was pleased by the fact that I could open the garden door at night and sneak my animals inside.

As well as teaching, Faith did all the cooking. We didn't serve lunches but we always put on a three-course dinner and there were days when Faith was so tired she'd fall asleep in the middle of a piano lesson.

As for the guests, I soon learned about them too. Apart from a quiet little man who wore a crumpled linen suit and lived in two rooms at one end of the veranda, working there all day and half the night with a pile of ledgers and a calculator, there were no permanent guests. The girls who crowded on the veranda in the evenings were mostly nurses from the army hospital thirty miles back in the bush. They stayed at The Bananas on their days off then returned to their quarters at the army camp. They paid cash for their accommodation but the young male guests didn't pay at all. They were university students from Brisbane who came up the coast to surf whenever they could snatch time away from lectures. Victor had an arrangement with them that in lieu of board they'd do the mowing and weeding and look after the tennis court but it seemed to me they did little of that. When they weren't at the beach they spent their time in the garage standing around the old Jaguar Victor was restoring. Looking back I'd say they paid him by keeping him company and by allowing him to pretend he was one of them. Indeed he was more the undergraduate than they. In the evenings he wore a striped blazer and a long cream scarf and his conversation was peppered with out-of-date slang. I can't think of a time I heard him call a female anything but doll. It used to make me laugh to hear him use the word for the big sweating Queensland women who brought their daughters to The Bananas for piano lessons.

Victor was too busy being a seaside college warden to his surfing chums to do much dentistry. In the time I was at the hotel, I don't suppose he saw more than one patient a week. I think it's fair to say he kept the dentist's chair in the bathroom more as a character prop than anything else. The university brigade spent a lot of time in there drinking rum and making false teeth. They liked making vampire teeth which they fitted over their own and wore until they grew tired of them.

The money Faith earned obviously kept the place going though I doubt it kept pace with the food and grog the young people got through.

As we wallowed into the full heat of summer, Faith went on wearing her black dress. She washed it out at night and put it on, still damp I'm sure, each morning. I asked her once why she wore a colour which drained so much of her beauty away. She told me she wore black because Victor liked her in it. The reason seemed a strange one in view of the fact that Victor always wore pastel colours himself — shirts of pink and white checks, or lemon and white, along with expensive linen trousers.

It seems to me that women who have a sister close to their own age get more fun out of life than others. Faith filled the role of sister for me and for months I thought I filled it for her. There was often an air of sadness about her but when we were alone together the sadness disappeared and she laughed a lot.

On the other hand, I didn't ever come to terms with the members of Victor's claque. They always seemed larger than life to me — perhaps because they displayed so much bare flesh. I suppose part of the truth is that I found their blatant masculinity unsettling and didn't come to terms with that.

Certainly their behaviour towards me was exemplary. They held my chair for me at the table, leapt to their feet to relieve me of heavy trays and, although I was at least twelve years older than they, always asked me if I wanted to be included when they made plans for surfing or sailing expeditions. But late in the evenings when the grog they'd imbibed began to show they sometimes turned their talk to Aborigines. They were not so pleasant then and listening to them I decided their senseless and unfair dislike of the black race was based on nothing more substantial than the fact that the Aborigines had refused to *vanish*. They told sick jokes about them, referring to them as Watermelons and Shoe Polish, names they must have learned from their fathers, for the words were a hangover from World War II when Queensland was virtually occupied by American troops.

From the moment the young men discovered how much their jokes upset me, they stopped telling them, at least in my presence. Instead they took to treating me as an engaging but slightly dotty aunt, and introduced me to newcomers as a radical writer from Pointy-Head Land.

Faith had a set of twins from an earlier marriage — Fiona and Laurel. Inevitably her daughters were known as the Big Twins and Little Twins. The older ones were sixteen and at boarding school where the fees were paid by Faith's father. Soon after I started at The Bananas they arrived home for the holidays and straightaway set about arranging a fancy dress party.

"Romance is the theme," they sang, "and you all have to come dressed appropriately."

11

At breakfast on the morning of the party, Victor jibbed at the idea of dressing up. "It's too hot," he said.

Without looking up from the toast I was buttering, I said, "You don't have to. Put a green paper carnation in the buttonhole of your blazer and come as Oscar Wilde."

There was a silence in the room that went on for so long I looked up to see why. Victor was staring at me. His neck was held rigid so that his head wobbled slightly with strain and his eyes, narrower than ever, were as hard to read as glass. I'm still not sure what that stare meant. I think it was a mixture of affront and temper, and because he wanted to reach out and slap me but wasn't game, impotence as well.

Part of me wanted to laugh and part of me wanted to tell him not to be an ass. Before I had a chance to do either, Victor scraped back his chair and getting to his feet said, "If you find that sod romantic, I can assure you I don't." Then he left the room. For the rest of the day he kept out of sight but he did make a token effort at dressing up for the party, appearing in the evening in a cream shirt and trousers and calling himself Dennis Lillee.

Faith had wanted to dress as Madam Butterfly. I talked

127

her into being the Little Mermaid instead. To keep it a secret she got ready in my room, putting on a sea-green body stocking and girdling her hips with fishnet and kelp. Then I threaded flowers and shells in her hair.

"You look breathtaking," I told her, surveying my handiwork. It was true. With her beauty and the little air of sadness she wore she was like an illustration from the fairy story.

By the time I'd helped Fiona and Laurel dress as George Sand and Chopin and the two little girls as characters from the Wizard of Oz, I had no time to finish my own costume. I'd planned to deck myself out in mosquito netting and float from my room as Dumas' Lady of the Camellias. Instead I borrowed Faith's black dress, combed my hair into a bang over my eyes and carried the soup in to dinner as Edith Piaf.

On the way I met Victor rushing along the main hall with bottles of wine. The sight of me in black made him stop.

"Are you trying to be funny?" he said.

I asked him what he meant.

"Dressing as Faith. Is it some kind of joke against the pair of us?"

"Don't be silly," I said, certain he was paying me back for my Oscar Wilde remark. And I brushed past him and went into the dining room, but looking back now, I think he came close to hitting the nail on the head. Unconsciously perhaps I *was* having a joke, but at his expense, not Faith's.

If Victor was annoyed when he saw my costume, he was livid when he saw his wife's. She came to dinner late, missing the soup course. She came carrying the meat. Laurel and Fiona were behind her with the vegetable dishes. As Faith emerged from the gloom of the hall with the girls attending her like handmaidens,

128

the ten people already seated started to clap. One of the claque, forgetting his role, cheered. Enjoying the moment, Faith paused before advancing and putting the meat in front of Victor. He didn't look at her. He'd stared hard enough when she was in the doorway but as she put the meat down and stood back for his approval, he turned to the girl on his right and said, "They've evolved a new substance for repairing teeth in America, you know. Tooth bonding, they call it. Apparently you rough the surface of the dicky tooth up a bit and trowel on the repair material the way you'd put plaster on a wall. It seems you can do anything with the stuff, fill in gaps, build up corners or resurface the whole tooth if you want to."

For a few moments Faith stayed where she was, but as Victor went on talking to the girl beside him, she turned and keeping her eyes down, went to the other end of the table. Throughout the meal, Victor ignored her. He was drinking heavily, draining his glass at a gulp and refilling it immediately. Usually when he drank he became boisterous. That night as he drank he became quiet. And every so often when Faith was looking the other way he shot at her the same kind of furious stare he'd given me at breakfast time.

Faith, for her part, was quiet too. She had patches of unaccustomed colour on her cheeks and as the meal progressed, the colour grew brighter.

Before long the rest of us stopped talking. Although the table was decorated with candles and frangipanni and although the Duchess of Windsor and Fred Astaire were there I can safely say it was the most unromantic dinner party of my life.

When I went to the kitchen with Laurel to get the strawberries Romanoff, Faith stole away to her bedroom. She came back to the dining room with the flowers and shells gone from her hair and wearing an old black dress she'd unearthed from her wardrobe. No one commented, least of all Victor, but for the rest of the meal I noticed he had a tiny smile at the corners of his mouth.

Later, when Faith and I were stacking the dishes, I said to her, "You have to stick up for yourself in this life, you know. It's a kind of social requirement people expect of you, like odourless breath."

She knew what I meant. I could tell that by the way she folded her lips a little as I spoke. But she sidestepped the issue by saying, "It was a delicious meal tonight, wasn't it? Just the right amount of garlic with the roast and the strawberries were perfect."

It was after eleven when she and I joined the others on the front veranda. Both tired, we lay in deck chairs to soak up the balm of the scented, starry night. I closed my eyes. No sooner had I done so than Faith nudged me. I opened them again to see an MG driven by Timothy Grimwade, a third year theology student who wore his hair parted in the middle like an old-time music-hall villain, fly up the drive and park on the lawn. In the back of the car was an electric piano.

It took Timothy's mates on the veranda no time at all to get the piano out of the car. Their idea was to rush it up to where we were sitting, but Timothy had other plans. Indicating a place on the lawn beside the steps, he had the piano put there. Victor had already sent someone to the garage for electrical leads and someone else for Faith's piano stool. When everything was in place, Timothy sat to play. He flexed his hands, beamed at us and launched into a medley of tunes from *My Fair Lady*.

Altogether the sights and sounds of the day had been too much for me. Timothy was the last straw. I began to giggle and knowing that Laurel and Fiona would join in if they saw me, I got to my feet and crept down to sit alone on the bottom step.

At the end of his bracket of numbers, Timothy stood up. He moved a little way from the piano and, for all the world as if he were on a concert platform, bowed then waited for applause. He didn't get any. His audience was too busy staring at the figure which came through the hibiscus hedge on Timothy's left and strode towards the piano. It was the man I'd heard whistling "Ave Maria" outside the Catholic church.

Victor was around in the bathroom drinking rum at the time. If he'd been on the veranda, no doubt he'd have put a stop to what happened next. As it was, the rest of us watched agog as the stranger said to Timothy, "I was walking past and heard the music." He waved a hand at the piano. "May I?" Then without waiting for a reply he sat down and began to play. He played some Chopin waltzes then some well-known pieces from opera. His playing was showy but good, so good in fact the notes seemed to fill the night and fall around us like jewels or stars or little pieces of the moon.

Faith tiptoed down to join me on the bottom step. Fiona followed her, and Mr Dunne, who lived at the end of the veranda, left his calculator and stood outside his door to listen.

The stranger, lost in the music, played on and on. He played for perhaps forty minutes. Then, when I at least thought the concert would last forever, he stood, and choosing my face out of all the ones watching, said, "The piano is not my instrument, of course. I studied it only until I was sixteen. I play the balalaika. Tomorrow night I will bring it."

He began to walk away. Faith stopped him by calling out, "Are you Russian?"

Turning, he found my face again, "I am Jan Tadic — Jugoslav," he said. Then he vanished through the hedge of hibiscus bushes.

Silence! I suppose at first none of us was certain any of it had happened.

Fiona broke the spell by saying, "Vinnie, you knew him. Who was it?"

"I've no idea."

"But he spoke to you — twice!"

"I saw him once outside the church. It was only for a moment. He wouldn't have remembered me."

"But he did. I could tell." Fiona's sixteen-year-old eyes were foolish with excitement. "I bet he fell in love with you and found out where you live."

Giving her a push I told her not to be silly but I must admit that from then on until we went to bed we talked of nothing but the Jugoslav.

"He could play, couldn't he?" said Laurel, "I mean really play?"

"Yes, he played like a professional," said Faith and squeezing my arm, told me what a dark horse I was.

By the next afternoon we'd learned a lot about Jan Tadic. We learned it from Loretta Burns, a nurse from our local one-sister hospital. Loretta had dropped into the hotel after lunch and hearing Jan's name told us she'd met him during her last stint on night shift. Fascinated by him, she'd made what amounted to a mental dossier on the man. He was married, she said, to a pretty Italian girl called Emilia, and as Faith had guessed was a professional musician. For over a year he'd played the balalaika in night clubs and hotels at most of the tourist resorts further down the coast. In fact he'd literally worked his way along the coast, being sacked from one job after another for causing trouble with other members of the staff. According to Jan, the

132

trouble was usually precipitated by his refusal to join the Musicians' Union but later his wife told Loretta there was more to it than that. She said that Jan was arrogant about his musicianship and that after a few glasses of Slivovic liked to tell his fellow employees the closest Australians got to making music was when an Aborigine blew through a didgeridoo. A fight often followed the remark, sometimes with the patrons joining in and before long Jan was unable to get a job anywhere along the coast. Finally, on the dole and with very little money, he and Emilia came to The Estuary and moved into the caravan park.

On the night Loretta met him, Emilia claimed to have been bitten on the hand by a funnel-web spider. She was too distressed, Loretta said, to make much sense, but apparently she and Jan had quarrelled in their caravan and Emilia, rushing off to bed in tears, had been bitten by a spider lurking in the bed clothes.

The hospital staff, unable to find any puncture marks on her hand, assured her there were no funnel-web spiders along that part of the coast. On hearing that Emilia became hysterical and in desperation the nurses sedated her and put her to bed. After sleeping for ten hours she woke in the best of spirits and went off in a taxi with her husband talking and laughing as if quarrels and spiders were things that didn't exist.

When Loretta had gone the rest of us made bets on the likelihood of Jan's turning up that night. Victor, who'd caught only the tail-end of the piano recital, pooh-poohed the idea, telling us we were behaving like children and that the Jugoslav had better things to do with his time than play music for half a dozen empty-headed dolls. He was wrong. A little after nine, Jan arrived, walking boldly up the drive with a balalaika case in his hand.

133

Apparently we weren't the only ones who'd been doing detective work; the first thing Jan did on reaching the veranda was single out Victor and then Faith. He introduced himself to them in a charming and rather formal manner, and after bowing to me as well took the balalaika from its case.

For a while he sat with his head on one side and tuned the instrument. Then he began to play. He played brilliantly, drowning us in music which was wild and sweet. The first things — his show pieces probably — were unfamiliar but soon he began to play cabaret songs like "Yesterday" and "La Vie en Rose". Many were tunes I'd danced to years before and moved by memory I went to the veranda rail and looked across the frangipannis to the estuary.

A path of water showed the moon's reflection. The rest of the river was dark. As I watched, a sloop, its sails furled and the engine running softly, moved through the stretch of bright water. It had no lights and as it slid on and disappeared I asked myself who'd be mad enough to sail that way at night. A drug-runner, I decided, straining my eyes to see, but the sloop had gone and I stood there feeling lonely in spite of the music and the crowd behind me.

Fiona brought me back to earth by tugging at my arm. "He's got a pale blue fingernail," she said, "Just one. Come and look."

I hardly heard her and she said again, "Jan's got a blue fingernail. It's weird." Then squeezing my arm the way her mother had done the night before, she added, "The rest of him's just gorgeous, though."

I followed her back to where Jan was playing and looking down at his hands saw that he did indeed have one pale blue fingernail. It was the nail on the third finger of his right hand. I looked then at his face and, still half dreaming, was moved by the beauty of silken eyelashes against masculine skin. Ashamed of my silliness, I turned away.

Again that night Jan played for a long time. Between numbers, Victor, who'd convinced himself that Jan was a communist spy with a couple of hand grenades suspended inside his trousers, plied him with vodka. Each time he handed Jan a drink he asked him to play some of his national songs. I suppose he thought he'd launch into "The Internationale" and give the game away. Late in the evening Jan did play and sing some Slavonic songs, while Victor, who'd drunk a lot of vodka too, glared at him from the back of the crowd. The young people danced a kind of jig to the folksongs and when they stopped to catch their breath Jan announced that he'd play some pieces he'd written himself.

His songs had intricate little melodies, some so sweet and sad we made him translate the words and teach them to us. My favourite was about a girl he'd met on the Isle of Crete.

Sybil came home from the mountains,
Casting a spell that drove the salt from the shore.
Her mother bloomed with love.
Her father celebrated — fell down and broke his balalaika.
Sybil smiled.
She danced and sang and taught the dog to heel.
We danced too like flowers tossed by laughter.
Then Sybil left and the salt blew in from the sea again.

That night it seemed to me Jan had put on a new personality. The remote man who'd been interested only in music had gone and in his place was a seasoned nightclub entertainer who enjoyed his ability to charm as much as his ability to play. None of the girls could take their eyes from him. For that matter, neither could I, and

135

watching him as he played and sang and flirted, I was forced to ask myself if my moment of being the lone voyager at the veranda rail had been the surfacing of a desire to build a downy little nest and furnish it with a balalaika player. Not wanting to ponder on that piece of self-analysis, I asked Jan to play a tango and when he did I rushed off to dance it with one of the surfing brigade.

The evening ended when Victor passed out with his face down on the billiard table. When that happened, Jan packed his balalaika away, bowed to the rest of us and walked slowly but steadily down the drive.

He came back on Wednesday night and again on Saturday. On the Saturday he brought his wife with him.

Emilia was twenty-five, with dark hair and big restless eyes. She held her head high, moving it around a lot and looking at her I was reminded of a deer scenting the air.

While Jan tuned his balalaika, Emilia sat next to Victor's feet on the end of the chaise longue. Tilting her head from side to side she admired her sandals — beaded ones with high wooden soles, then suddenly she turned to Victor and said, "I'm tired tonight. I'm menstruating. When I menstruate I lose a lot of blood and feel faint. Always I have heavy periods and always I suffer with them."

Victor cast a wild look around for Faith and not finding her, hoisted himself out of the chaise longue and disappeared into the hotel. Happily, Emilia settled herself where he'd been sitting and didn't move until I took Jami and Peta inside to put them to bed. Then, to my surprise, she followed us to the bathroom we used. Without speaking she watched from the doorway while the twins brushed their teeth. When they'd finished I shooed them out and as I moved to leave the room myself, Emilia stepped in front of me and asked for a drink of water.

I hesitated then turned back and rinsed out the toothbrush glass.

She watched me over the rim as she drank and as she handed the glass back, she said, "I came here tonight because I wanted to meet you."

"Me?" I pantomimed surprise.

"I have heard nothing but Vinnie, Vinnie, for a week, so I came to look at you myself."

Not knowing how to respond, I kept quiet.

"My husband thinks you're a very fascinating woman."

Brushing past her, I said, "He's teasing you. I hardly know him." And I followed the children to their bedroom.

Emilia came too. Again without speaking she watched as I tucked in the girls and kissed them, but when I walked across to turn off the light she reached out and taking the tip of my shirt collar between her fingers, said, "Vinnie Beaumont, do you know what I think? I think it's very clever of you to dress all the time like Mick Jagger." Then, turning on her wooden soles, she left me and walked away along the corridor.

To say I was taken aback is to put it mildly. Emilia had given me the old cooler and no mistake. For the life of me I couldn't see why. When I told her I hardly knew her husband I'd been speaking the truth. Altogether we'd spoken no more than a dozen sentences to each other, short ones at that. I told myself that Emilia's broadside was just a shot in the dark; that she'd come to The Bananas to find out what brought Jan there and finding herself alone with someone had been unable to resist planting a territorial flag. Immediately after that piece of rationalisation, I reminded myself that Emilia

137

had been alone with me because she'd made it her business to be, and then I began to wonder if all along I'd been giving off tiny signals of interest in Jan, signals he'd had no trouble in reading.

As Emilia's shapely bottom disappeared around the corner of the corridor, I must have laughed, because one of the twins asked sleepily what the joke was.

"Just me," I said, "I'm the joke," and went back to tuck them in again.

For the rest of that night I kept away from both Jan and Emilia, seating myself at the other end of the veranda, and when Jan called me and asked me to join in the singing of one of his songs, I smiled at him and went inside to make coffee instead.

During the next week, on an afternoon when Jami and Peta were out with their mother, Victor called me to the garage and asked me to help for a few minutes with his old Jag. He showed me a wire to hold, then hurried around to the other side of the car and while he fiddled with the engine, said, "The Big Twins tell me you stop each day and talk to the gang of cut-throats who live on the pier."

"They're not cut-throats. They're kids without jobs, that's all."

We were talking about the young people who'd set up house in the old picture theatre at the end of the pier. Five of them lived there permanently and half a dozen came and went.

Still fiddling with the engine, Victor said, "You're just like my sister, Liz. All art and socialism — not a brain in your head. Those kids as you call them have set themselves to undermine our society. You can see that by the way they dress. One of them, the one with the orange hair, has the words 'My Mother got me from a Real Prick' painted on his jacket."

Caught halfway between amusement and despair, I laughed and Victor, furious, said, "If you think that's funny, you shouldn't be looking after two little girls."

"I'm not supposed to be looking after them. I'm supposed to be the bookkeeper."

Ignoring the remark, Victor said, "You think it's right, do you, for children to see things like that?"

I took my time in answering, "Probably not, but I don't think it's right either to shield them from the fact that there are other children in this country who have no jobs, no homes and no hope."

"Children be damned! They're what I called them before, cut-throats. I've seen them marching out onto the pier, as large as life, with their arms full of stolen property. Todd West, the police constable, told me they've got the place done up like the Ritz with stuff they've shoplifted. Potplants and deck chairs for heaven's sake, just as if they'd earned them. It's obscene. They should be in jail."

"Give them time and they will."

"And drugtaking! They're right into that, you know. They steal food and furniture then blow their dole cheques on heroin. I tell you, if we don't do something about that lot, they'll bring this country to its knees."

"Victor, the drug that'll bring this country to its knees is the one you keep in the bathroom cupboard. And I don't mean the dental supplies."

For a while Victor was too angry to answer and when he did his voice was shaking. "Just understand this, Madam, when you're in charge of my children, you'll keep well clear of the pier and the scum that lives on it. Do you hear me?"

"Yes, I hear you and I'll do as you say as long as *you* understand that when I'm on my own and I meet those kids I'll stop and speak to them as I do now." Somehow

I managed to keep my voice calm, but by then I was pretty furious myself and when I finished speaking, I let go of the wire I was holding and walked from the garage.

As I went I felt Victor's eyes boring maliciously into my back. I didn't care. Mixed with my anger was a feeling of relief because I'd finally shed some of the protective colouring I'd assumed for the benefit of the Bogles.

12

I was in my room, wearing my old silk kimono, and do-ing breathing exercises on the floor while I waited for the children to come home. A knock, so soft I wasn't certain I'd heard it, sounded on the door. I waited and when it came again, called, "Come in." The door opened and Jan Tadic came into the room.

For a moment I was too surprised to realise who it was and when I did, I leapt to my feet and pulled the sash of my kimono tight.

Neither of us spoke. I was conscious of my tousled hair, my bare legs and feet. While we faced each other a movement outside the door caught my eye. Victor was standing in the hallway watching. Without giving myself time to think, I crossed to the door and shut it.

In shutting Victor out of course, I'd shut Jan in. I looked at him. In my narrow room, he seemed taller than I'd thought and with his stiff black hair and high cheekbones, more foreign too. Not knowing what he'd come for, I had a wild moment of imagining myself in a crushing Slavonic embrace while Victor's ear was glued to the other side of the door. Then Jan moved and I saw the parcel he'd been holding behind him. It was a brown paper bag with "Coles New World" printed on it. My fantasy evaporated. Waving a hand towards the sagging armchair at the other end of the room, I said, "Have a seat."

Jan hesitated and I added, "It's okay. Billie will chaperone us." (The dog had already appeared from the shade of the lilies outside and was hurrying in to sniff suspiciously at Jan's trousers.)

I told her to sit and when she'd satisfied herself there was no cause for alarm, she stretched out on the floor between us. Keeping a wary eye on her, Jan went to the chair and sat, putting his supermarket bag carefully by his feet.

I perched myself on the end of the bed and waited to see what would happen.

Jan looked around him. He looked at my books and the prints and posters I'd tacked onto the walls. He took in the snaps of animals I'd owned and photographs of one or two people I'd loved along the way. Last of all he looked at my desk. I looked at it too — saw pens and pencils in a pottery mug, saw the bunch of everlastings picked in the forest near Maryston and saw the Tom Waits record I'd stood the teapot on the day before. In the middle of it all was my old typewriter with a pair of sneakers on it.

Something about the desk seemed to reassure Jan. His forehead relaxed and it was only then that I realised he'd been frowning slightly since coming into the room.

He still didn't speak though, and deciding it was up to me to break the ice, I said, "I call my room the Star-Ship Maryston — so welcome aboard."

"Why do you call it that?"

"Star-Ship because when I'm alone in here, I can fly anywhere I want to; Maryston because that's where I come from. And what about you, Jan? Where do you come from? Jugoslavia? Or are you a Russian spy as Victor thinks?"

Laughing and looking younger, he stretched his legs out and was at ease. "I'm Jugoslav," he said. "That's something I want to talk to you about."

"Your English is very good — perfect really."

"Ah — that's another thing I want to talk about." He flourished a packet of cigarettes. "May I? Will you?"

I shook my head and after he'd lit a cigarette, he said, "I wish to tell you about myself. I was born in a little town on the Adriatic. A village really, not a town. A village where everyone thought they had the right to know how many fleas your dog had. A village where the priests trailed around in long black dresses and gossiped like midwives." Jan frowned and was lost on the other side of the world.

"Yes?" I prompted.

He came back, focused his gaze on the end of his cigarette and said, "My father was an English army officer. A captain. He was stationed in our town towards the end of the war. He worked with the partisans."

"As a liaison officer?"

"Yes, that's right. Well, he met my mother and they fell in love. She became pregnant and to the surprise of everyone in that stinking little village, he married her. The time came, of course, when he was ordered back to England. My mother waited for him to send for us, but he never did. He sent money, plenty of it. He sent enough for me to be educated, but he didn't send for us. My mother, crazy fool, believed he would. She went on believing it when anyone with brains would have given up. She had me taught the piano because my father had played it and she had me taught English so I'd be ready for the life in England when we got there. She learned to speak it too. We used to study the dictionary — Webster's was the one we had. We tried to learn a page of it every night. When we were halfway through, I'd

143

had enough and ran away. After that I used my grand-father's name of Tadic."

"And the balalaika?"

"There were Russians in our town as well as English-men. They didn't mix with us but two of them were billeted across the street from where my mother and I lived. One had a balalaika and in the evenings he'd play it. One of my earliest memories is of the late summer sun, pigeons whirring overhead and the sound of the balalaika. I loved it — it spoke to me. I stopped study-ing the piano when I ran away, but the first time I had money of my own I bought a balalaika and after that, whenever I could find a teacher, I took lessons."

"When you left home, where did you go?"

"I stowed away on a boat and got across to Italy. I had no passport, you understand, and very little money. I was caught the day I landed. The bastards jailed me for a week then sent me home. I ran away again almost immediately, but I'd learned something in between and I worked for a few weeks before I crossed to Italy a second time. I still had no passport and I was caught again but after the payment of a little bribe or two I got away. It went on like that for seven years. I lived all around the Adriatic, in and out of jail, often on the run. Sometimes I worked as a waiter, sometimes as a clerk. Now and then I played the piano in lousy little bars, but, ah, my heart was always with the balalaika and always I returned to it."

Jan drew hard on his cigarette then flipped it out into the garden. "When I was twenty-three I found out women liked me." He was watching me with eyes which had become Asiatic and unreadable. "It's sad I didn't realise it before, but when I did, I decided to capitalise on the fact. From then on, I made my living out of women." He spread his hands and still watching me, said, "I made my living as a gigolo."

144

Jan was still. He was waiting, I knew, to gauge my reaction. But I wasn't ready to give one — I was too busy trying to fit onto Jan the picture the word gigolo gave me of a dinner-suited young man with round moist eyes and a Jazz Age haircut.

In the end I ducked the issue by asking about his blue fingernail.

The question delighted him. He laughed loudly and said, "Ah — you noticed."

"One could scarcely fail. Is it hurt, or painted or what?"

"Not painted — repaired — resurrected, one could say. I play music with my nails as you know and to break one is a disaster. When it happens I always try to find the severed piece and if I do, I stick it back with glue and toilet paper. This time the roll of paper was blue." Jan laughed again.

He must've seen disbelief on my face, "I'm not telling you a little furphy," he said, looking proud of his Australian word. "To mend your nail with glue and toilet paper is an old musicians' trick. I doubt they do it in the Berlin Philharmonic but perhaps they do. Anyway, I'll tell you how to do it. First you coat the nail with glue and attach the broken piece. Then you shape the toilet paper to fit and stick it on. When it's dry, you put on many more coats of glue and in the end, ha — it's as tough as you could wish. Look!"

Jan came across the room and thrust his hand in front of my face.

I looked at the nail and then at his hand. It was beautiful — long-fingered and slim but muscular as well. Then the thought of myself growing weak at the sight of a self-confessed gigolo's hand was too much for me and I began to laugh.

Through the laughter, I said, "Were you really a gigolo?"

"Yes, that's not a little furphy either. Look, it's all in here." Jan shot back to where he'd left his parcel. The quick movement worried Billie who growled and got to her feet. For a few moments there was confusion in the room. That made me laugh even more and I wondered what Victor was making of all the merriment if he was silly enough to be still listening in the hall.

Jan made it safely back to the bed and taking a book the size of a photo album out of his brown paper bag, presented it to me.

"It's all in here," he said. "I wrote it down, everything, from the day I left home until I married Emilia. This one's the first volume. I have another one at the caravan park. I'd like to publish them of course. The problem is that when I write, something happens to my English. It becomes ornate, or stilted — I don't know." He shrugged.

"Something is wrong with the way I write and I need help. Faith told me you're a writer. Is that true?"

"In a way it is."

"Then I would like you to read my story and tell me what you think. If you like it — if you think it worthwhile, perhaps you could . . . " Jan stopped there and didn't finish.

"Edit it?"

"Yes, yes. Something like that," said Jan and giving Billie a wide berth went back to the chair.

I looked at the book. On the front of it, he'd pasted a pen and wash drawing of a young man with a balalaika case in his hand hurrying down the street towards a harbour. The text inside wasn't typed but written by hand in slanting Gothic script. It was done in black ink, the down-strokes elongated and as parallel as rain. I flipped through the pages. The writing didn't vary, from one end of the book to the other, it was tall and black and sloping. Every so often there was a drawing of the young man with the balalaika case. In one of them, looking surprised, he was standing in a rowboat with a load of Jewish emigrants, in another he was on horseback and in the company of a woman whose face I recognised because I'd seen it more than once on the gossip page of *Time Magazine*. It belonged to an American socialite who'd had four husbands, one of them an ambassador.

Holding the page up so Jan could see, I said, "Were you *her* houseboy too?"

"For a little while." He gave a shrug. "We quarrelled and she kicked me out. That was part of the pattern. As I told you, I lived all around the Adriatic — in Italy, on Crete and Rhodes. Sometimes I even got as far as Lebanon. I lived with many different women. Some of them were famous, some beautiful, some merely rich. It doesn't matter what they are though, in the end they always kick you out."

I stared at Jan and tried to imagine him playing the gigolo on the beach in Beirut. To my surprise the thought caused me a needle-prick of jealousy so I abandoned it and returned to the book. Starting at the beginning, I concentrated on the Gothic script and read:

The day I left home was the day I gave up God. My mother was crying and the wind was conveying a scent both aromatic and tender from the mountains down into the town. I left home in a taxi, the dilapidated squeaking old black Dodge that had served our town for thirty years or more. It still had on its back the rusted gas-producer it had worn through the long years of the war.

The taxi driver tried to seduce me on the way to the harbour. I was sixteen and he a man of fifty-five with several grandchildren and a voluminous wart on his nose. He drove me to an empty warehouse and the tenor of his talk on the way made me sick. There was nothing for me to do but flee the taxi and run, leaving behind my cardboard suitcase. That's when I gave up God. I gave Him up when I gave up my suitcase.

147

I was soon in a fight at the waterfront. I had to fight two toughs who laughed at my woollen suit. In a matter of minutes the suit was torn and dusty. I lost too the knife I was carrying, but a girl rescued me. She was the sister of one of my assailants. Her face was porcine but she was kind. She hid me in her room for three lengthy days and nights while I waited for a boat. We drank red wine and ate onion soup. I'll never forget that girl; she was dirty and she had diarrhoea, but her heart was the gentle heart of a Madonna; she succeeded in turning upside down many of the old-fashioned notions I had had about women. On one hand I had the picture of my mother with her little lace collars and her religion, who'd conceived a child — me — out of wedlock. On the other, that girl with her kind heart and soiled knickers who helped me get away.

I stopped reading but I didn't look up from the page because I was dying to laugh, had been since I got as far as the girl's porcine face. I steadied myself by trying to work out what I could say to Jan.

"Don't laugh," I told myself, "because if you do, he'll never forgive you. Don't pile on the criticism either. Just be encouraging and save the rest till later."

By then I'd sobered enough to look across at Jan and say, "It starts off with gusto and the drawings are charming. Some of the words are — well, unusual. I'm sure you know that, and anyway, books always have to be reworked. Is this the first draft you've done?"

"The *only* draft. I don't like rewriting. It bores me. Once every few months I like to sit and write in one long inspired burst. I may write night and day for three weeks, then, poof, I'm finished. I try to write like Hemingway because I admire his work. Perhaps I am mistaken to do that. Perhaps I should work more slowly and change things. Make them . . . " Jan pulled a face, "prettier. Emilia thinks so anyway."

"No, I don't agree with that. Look, I'll read it through and then we'll talk again."

148

"Yes, that's what I was hoping for. You'll find, of course, much more than I've told you. I've done many things in life — carried cocaine to Catania and banknotes out of Istanbul. I lived with a titled woman on Lesbos and with a cabaret star in Greece. I put it all down. I didn't even change the names."

"Well you'll have to. You might have to rewrite a lot of it but the real test will be when you send it to a publisher."

Jan put his fingers to his lips and made a little kissing sound. "Vinnie," he said, "all my life, I've been looking for a woman like you, and here, at the very end of the earth, I've found you."

Holding his eyes with mine, I said, "You can put the gigolo act back in the cupboard, old buddy. If I help you, it'll be because I like your book, not because you charmed me into it."

Tough talk and I wasn't sure even then that it was true. The words made Jan laugh though. "There, you see," he said, "I find the woman of my dreams and the paradox is that she has the power to see straight through me."

I changed the subject by asking where he'd met Emilia and how long they'd been married.

He said, "We met in Rome. Emilia was the script girl with a film crew making documentaries. They booked into the hotel where I was living with Lois, the American woman you saw in the drawing. We'd had a fight, Lois and I. She gave a lunch party for some crooks and poseurs and instead of being there to pour martinis I went to a little bar and got drunk. I came back late in the afternoon to find Lois had locked me out of her suite. She'd put my belongings in the corridor — the only thing she kept was my balalaika. I was furious. I rushed out into the street and got up to her rooms by way of the

149

balcony. When Lois saw me she tried to break the balalaika across my back and in retaliation I took her clothes from the wardrobe and poured wine over them. Things got out of hand and someone sent for the police. Emilia arrived at the hotel in time to see me being marched through the foyer in handcuffs. I was taken to the police station and charged with assault. At the hotel Emilia asked what had happened. Naturally the staff was full of chatter-chatter-chatter. Emilia heard many things, most of them exaggerations, but the short and long of it was that she came to the police station the next morning to see if she could help me."

"And you fell in love and married her," I said in Fiona's singsong voice.

"No. No. No. It was not that simple. How could it be? Emilia was sweet and shy and unspoilt but alas she had no money. Also, by then Lois had relented. She paid my fine and took me back. By the time she kicked me out again, Emilia had left Rome and I didn't know where she'd gone."

"How did you find her?"

"We kept bumping into each other. It was strange. I'd be in Athens and I'd meet her on a bus. Or I'd be in a cafe in Trieste and she'd be at the next table. It became a joke between us and we started communicating by postcard. Of course I tried to seduce her many times, but always I failed. I have to tell you this about my wife — of all the women I had known, she was the only one who had virtue, the only one who was not a whore underneath her manners and her smiles."

"And smart with it," I said but only to myself.

"One Easter I was in Venice and down on my luck. I had flu and no money for medicines let alone my room. Emilia found me there and looked after me. During my convalescence we talked and talked. Emilia asked me to give up my bad ways and settle down. To tell you the truth I felt it was time to have a woman of my own and somewhere permanent to live. I was tired of asking patronesses for pocket money and tired of fawning like a little dog, so when I was well again I got work as a musician. After that Emilia came to my bed, but she wouldn't ever stay with me. I'd wake in the morning and find her gone. She wanted me to give up music too — to do something respectable, like going to work every day at a bank."

"And did you?"

"No, I didn't go that far. I kept telling Emilia I would though. In a way it was funny. She'd find me jobs and I'd ruin the interview. She worked out, of course, what I was doing and we quarrelled a lot. We'd meet and make love and argue and part. Things went on that way for two years, with Emilia growing thinner all the time. She was not eating and not sleeping. Then she told me she had a spot on the lung. That frightened me. I'd come to rely on her; she was the core of my life, I suppose you could say. And when she asked me to come out here, I agreed. Plenty of jobs, we thought, and plenty of sun. So we married, because it was cheaper to travel that way."

There was silence in the room. Then Jan said, "When we got to Australia there were very few jobs. It's funny, isn't it, that after coming all this way our lives have hardly changed? The landscape's different, not much else."

"Your book might change everything."

"With your help — perhaps. I hope so. I would be pleased to have some . . . " Jan paused. "Some honour."

Our tête-à-tête ended there because Jami and Peta burst into the room demanding to be taken for a swim.

Raising my voice above theirs, I told Jan I'd read his manuscript as soon as I could. He blew me a kiss, ruffled the hair of the twins and left.

At The Bananas that night we had more people to dinner than usual and it was after one o'clock when I got to bed. Although I was exhausted, I settled myself under the mosquito net to read Jan's book. The slanting black letters moved around in front of my eyes and I fell asleep before I'd finished the first page.

13

For the next couple of days I carried the book around the hotel with me, dipping into it whenever I got the chance. Victor, seeing it on the office table, picked it up at one stage and read a few paragraphs. He closed it and put it down, gave me one of his glassy stares and left the room without a word.

As for me, once I'd got used to the Gothic script and quasi-literary style, I enjoyed Jan's story. It was fresh and funny, at times heart-warming because of its simplicity, at others shocking because of the things it dealt with. Now and then the action was held up by descriptive passages which I found boring, and some of the things he said about women were unfair. Nevertheless, I was certain that edited and typed, the manuscript would be snapped up by a publisher.

Needless to say I was anxious to pass my opinion on to Jan but for the rest of the week he stayed away from the hotel. By then we'd slid into a heatwave so unbearable even the locals complained. The sea breeze had abandoned us and day after day the air was hot and still. At the beach we huddled under a striped umbrella and went swimming in floppy cotton hats and long-sleeved shirts. I was there with the children on Saturday when the breeze began to blow again. It blew gently at first then in long menacing gusts which piled water against the jetty and sent a squadron of clouds across the sun.

"It's going to rain like fury," I called to the children. "We'd better go."

Laden with the umbrella and the rest of our gear, we struggled up the bank and across the no-man's-land between the beach and the road. We were stopped there by a procession. Although it was neither Anzac nor Remembrance Day, the procession was headed by a kilted piper in front of an old-fashioned car with three World War I veterans in it. I looked at the heroes. They were so old their eyes had returned to the rounded innocence of boyhood.

What do they think about? I asked myself. The past or death or what?

Impulsively I whistled to them and when one turned his stiff old neck I waved and he waved back.

Twenty men from World War II went by with their battalion flag. They were followed by half a dozen sea scouts and some lads from the local surf lifesaving club. Last of all came a detachment of school children wearing coloured sashes. To the strains of "Scotland the Brave" the little procession passed us, turned right at the corner and marched in the direction of the town square.

As soon as it seemed polite to move, the children and I crossed the road and hurried towards the hotel. I was struggling with the gate when the storm caught us. Within a minute we were drenched by rain so heavy it turned the garden trees to ghosts. Inside the gate the children put their heads down and ran. I spent a few moments trying to put the beach umbrella up, decided against it and followed them. At the bottom of the steps I looked up. Sitting on the chaise longue out of reach of the rain was Emilia Tadic. Her clothes were the ones she'd worn the night I met her, but for some reason she'd added a pair of white crocheted mittens which were very much like the things people used to put on sauce bottles to make them decent for the dinner table.

Before I reached the top of the steps, Emilia stood up and said, "I've come for my husband's book."

It was hard to hear her over the sound of the rain on the roof. That didn't matter. I guessed what she'd said — had known, I think, what she'd come for in the first moment of seeing her.

Out of breath I stooped to put my burdens on a dry part of the floor. Then straightening, I pushed back my wet hair and said, "The book's great. We must talk about it."

"I haven't come to talk," said Emilia.

"Please — I'll get the kids dry and then make coffee." I spoke at the same time as Peta asked what Emilia had done to her hands.

"Nothing." I told her. "She's wearing mittens."

"They look silly," said Peta.

"You're being rude. Go round to the bathroom and take off your swimsuit. You can wrap yourself in a towel and I'll be with you in a minute."

Sensing that I was already on edge, Peta said, "Can we go to Father's bathroom and have a drink of vodka?"

"Certainly not. Go to your own bathroom and if we get a few manners back in our lives, banana thickshakes might be on the menu."

Peta hesitated, but I'd won the round. Giving her a push, Jami said, "Come on, Pete," and the two little girls rushed inside.

To Emilia, I said, "Do you mind coming to the bathroom while I attend to the children?"

"I don't want to wait," she said. "I just want the book."

"Did Jan ask you to come for it?"

155

"Yes."

"Why didn't he come himself?"

"He's busy."

"But he must want to know what I think of it."

"Why should he?"

Not wanting to argue over the sound of the rain I motioned for Emilia to follow me into the billiard room. There we faced each other again and I said, "You don't understand. The book's good, possibly very good. If Jan rewrites it, I think it'll sell."

"The one who doesn't understand is you," said Emilia. "You're like all Australians. You live in this empty country where everyone thinks like a little child. Life's too easy for you. You don't know how hard it is to get things. You think because you had my husband in your bedroom all the afternoon . . . "

I interrupted to ask if Jan had told her that.

She said, "Yes", but her eyes, as bold as Peta's had been when she asked for vodka, wavered and I knew she was lying.

Victor, I thought. The bastard.

Emilia said, "Jan would not rewrite the book. That's something else you don't understand."

"I'd help him."

"He still wouldn't do it. He's too lazy. He likes to play music and talk and drink all day. I have had many years of that and worrying about it has taken my health away."

"I can't believe Jan's lazy. If he were, he wouldn't have written the book in the first place."

"Writing! What work is that? To sit at the table scratching all day with a pen like a schoolboy!"

"But Emilia. Jan's an artist — a musician. You knew that when you married him."

"None of that is your concern. Please get me the book."

156

I could see she wasn't going to give in, and telling myself there'd be plenty of time later to talk the matter over with Jan, I went to my room and came back with the book.

As I handed it to Emilia, I nodded towards the rain. "You can't go in this. Won't you stay for coffee?"

"I have a friend waiting at the side gate with a car." Emilia took the book and hugged it to her. Then looking me bang in the eye, she said, "Goodbye, Vinnie Beaumont." And she turned and went out the door.

That wasn't the end of it though, because at the top of the steps, she turned again and holding the book over her head so that the rain soaked the drawing on the cover, she called back to me, "He uses drugs — did you know that?"

Her words didn't surprise me. I was bright enough to know that a man like Jan would be sold on the Romantic Myth and all its connotations. What did surprise me was the look on Emilia's face when she told me. It was a mixture of hostility and cheekiness which reminded me again of Peta.

Sorry for her in spite of myself I stepped out onto the veranda but before I could speak Emilia turned once more, and although the steps were wet and slippery, hurried down them and disappeared in the direction of the side entrance.

The storm raged for three days, assaulting the hotel with rain which blotted out the river and wind which bent the trees horizontal. Victor told us we were on the edge of a cyclone and that the roof would go at any minute. Somehow it stayed on and by Tuesday night the storm was over.

The next morning Faith and I got up early to tackle the damage in the garden. We were still at breakfast when the phone rang. Faith answered it and came back to say Jan Tadic wanted to speak to me.

157

I had no premonition of what was going to happen and was smiling when I picked up the phone and said "Hallo."

Jan's voice came back. "Vinnie, I rang to say goodbye. I've very little time because we're leaving in a minute but I couldn't go without speaking to you first."

It took me a moment to make sense of what he'd said and when I did all I could find to say was, "I don't believe you." And I remember being surprised because my lips felt like someone else's.

"It's true, Vinnie. We're leaving now — this morning. Emilia was frightened by the storm and wants to go. Not only that, I have to take a job the CES has found me. It's only for a little while, then I'll be back and we'll work on the book."

I couldn't think of anything to say. I knew he wouldn't be back and stood with my head down staring at a stain on the carpet.

"Vinnie, are you still there?"

"Yes," I said through clumsy lips.

"Vinnie, don't be angry. I have no choice. If I don't take the job, I'll lose the dole. What will happen to me then?"

"What is it, anyway?" I said. "Playing the balalaika?"

"No, nothing like that."

"Are you going to be a clerk or something?"

"No, nothing like that either."

I heard someone, Emilia I suppose, calling Jan's name in the background.

"I must go," he said, "but I wanted to tell you something." The next words, a stream of them, were spoken in another language.

When I told Jan I didn't know what they meant, he said, "I spoke some lines from a song I wrote for you. It goes something like this — 'I searched all my life for the flower that grows high in the Alps, unattainable. When I found it, my heart knelt. And humbly, I left it there with the flower.' Vinnie, dearest Vinnie, goodbye."

I put the phone down with a hand that was hurting because it had been clenched so hard around the receiver. Then I tried to make a joke to myself about Jan's great line in goodbyes. Not able to find anything funny in it, I went to the front door and stared out into the ravaged garden.

Finding me there, Faith asked what had happened.

"Jan rang to say goodbye. He's leaving this morning with Emilia — going away."

"Where to?"

"He didn't say."

Faith was watching my face. "Take my car and go to the caravan park," she said. "You can stop him."

"Don't be mad. Jan Tadic has said goodbye to a thousand women and I'll bet not one ever stopped him leaving."

"You could."

"No, Faith, you overestimate me — I couldn't." Having said that, I went down to the garden and began to pick up the broken branches on the lawn.

Jan's departure plunged me into a depression where I found all my old griefs waiting for me. Faith and the members of Victor's claque set themselves to bring me out of it but nothing they did helped. In the end I decided to work the sorrow out of myself and spent a week washing the walls in my bedroom and painting them a rosy terracotta.

The day after I finished, Victor called me into the office. While Faith watched, he pointed to a carton on the table. "If it's work you want, there's plenty there," he said.

Inside the carton were bundles of used cheque books

bound together with rubber bands. Looking at them I guessed there were fifty or sixty books and because I'd seen such collections before, I said, "You haven't lodged your tax return."

"Got it in one," said Victor.

"You haven't lodged one for years."

"Spot on."

"How long since you did?"

"Eight years." Victor was frank-faced and smiling but his fingers beat a nervous little tattoo on the edge of the carton.

"Why did you leave it?"

"You know how it is. The first couple of years got away from me and after that I didn't know where to start."

Faith said, "We kept the bank statements and every receipt and invoice. They're all in boxes in our bedroom."

"Why didn't you ask Mr Dunne on the veranda to do it for you? He's some sort of accountant."

Instead of answering, Victor hummed and ha'd until I said, "You want me to do it, don't you?"

In unison, just as they'd done on the day I started at The Bananas, they said, "Would you?"

I told them I'd make up my mind when I'd seen the boxes in the bedroom so Faith took me there and showed me a row of cartons in the bottom of the wardrobe.

Having looked inside and seen dust and spider webs as well as papers, I straightened up and was about to say, "Not on your Nellie," but Faith caught my arm and said, "Please Vinnie — Victor's never agreed to have it done before. If you put him off now, he never will."

"It'd take me weeks."

Her eyes were locked on my face. "Please."

In the end I said I'd post the debits and credits into

ledgers as long as Victor promised that as soon as I was finished he'd take the lot to an accountant in Brisbane.

When he heard that, Victor rushed to the bathroom and came back with three glasses of planter's punch. "Here's to Vinnie," he said, lifting his glass. "The find of a lifetime."

I started on the papers that afternoon and many times in the weeks to come as I sat in the heat and stared at invoices for Beenleigh rum and cockroach baits I felt like putting a match to them, but I kept on, and finally the day came when I presented Victor with a record of his receipts and expenditure for the past eight years. He infuriated me by spending several days in looking for mistakes in my figures. Of course he found some and made a fuss about them, appearing every so often from the office with a pen behind his ear to tell me I'd missed bank charges of two dollars fifty or something similar incurred back in 1979. His auditing went on until it dawned on me he was merely putting off the day when he took the ledgers to Brisbane. I said as much to him and we had a God Almighty row which ended with my threatening to take the books myself.

Immediately Victor's temper vanished, "I knew you would," he crowed and went away whistling to work on his car.

I turned to Faith. "What's wrong with the man? What's he afraid of?"

She dropped her eyes.

"There's nothing wrong with the figures," I told her. "Victor hasn't done anything dodgy. The amount of money he's lost each year proves that."

Faith kept her eyes down and I thought, Jesus, Victor *is* frightened. That's why he hides here at the hotel with his undergrad mates. He's frightened of everything but most of all he's frightened of having to sit opposite some man who'll take one look at his books and know what a failure he is.

Having worked that out there was nothing for me to do but clap my hands cheerfully and say, "Okay, I'll take the books to Brisbane. I'll go on the bus. I'm dying for a day out anyway."

Faith wasn't taken in by my cheerfulness. She raised her mermaid eyes while I was speaking and when I'd finished, said, "Just make sure Victor gives you the money for the best lunch in town."

I caught the bus at six in the morning when the sky and the estuary were colourless and the headland in between was nothing but a brushstroke of black. Before long we left the coast and skirting foothills climbed slowly up into the silence of a rain forest. The sun came out while we were there and by sending a few shafts of light through the trees turned part of the forest into a stained-glass window.

From the hills we swooped into a valley of rich farms and breathtaking views. It was hot in the bus and became hotter when the driver pulled up to let a man on foot go by with six or seven sheep. We'd stopped beside a horse stud with the name "Dallas" written in king-size letters above the gate. The buildings were of Spanish design and every field and pasture, even the smallest of them, was separated from its neighbour by a sparkling white fence. More fence, a double row of it, ran along the road. It must take an army, I thought, to keep it painted.

Not far from the bus three workmen were putting up another fence. One of them, a fellow in a straw sombrero, picked up a post, dropped it in a hole and thumped it down once or twice. My mind, working at a snail's pace, registered the fact that he was wearing Jan Tadic's clothes.

The next moment my head was out the window and I was shouting, "Jan! Jan! It's me — Vinnie."

He let go of the post and taking his sombrero off, held it high.

"What are you doing?" I shouted.

"Working." He began to walk towards the bus.

"What about your music?"

The bus began to move.

"I'll get back to it."

We were picking up speed and I hung further out the window to shout, "And your book?"

"I'll get back to that too."

I had a dozen more questions to ask but already we were out of earshot and the only thing I could do was hang out the window and wave. Jan stayed by the fence, his hat held high until we were out of sight. It was only later when I was seated and facing the front again that I had time to realise his fingernails had been cracked and broken and his clothing soaked with sweat.

It was dark when we went past the stud farm on the way home that night. All I saw of it was a cluster of lights and the pattern of the fences.

During the week I thought of borrowing Faith's car on my day off and driving to the place where Jan worked. I didn't do it though because I knew that if I did, a foreman with a cowboy hat and a bull's-head buckle on his belt would tell me that on payday Jan had collected his wages and then he and Emilia had left for Rockhampton or Cairns or the other end of the Milky Way.

So the conversation from the bus was the last I ever had with Jan Tadic and to steal a line from one of his songs, the salt blew in from the sea again.

14

I woke one morning to find that the light pouring into my room had changed. It was greener than it had been the day before and on the ceiling there were brand new fans of shadow. I sat up and looking out into the garden, saw the space between my door and the fence had been filled with palm trees — hundreds of them, some three feet high, some seven, and all of them in pots. When I stepped outside to take a closer look I found they overflowed the space in front of my room and filled the recess between two wings of the hotel. I couldn't even guess where they'd come from, and leaving the dog and cat to a giddy game of hide and seek between the pots, I went back to my room, grabbed my kimono and set off for the kitchen to make some tea.

The hotel was quiet. It was Sunday and no more than half past six. The young people who'd booked in for the weekend had all been to a rugby club dance in Brisbane the night before and I knew none of them would stir till lunch time.

When I was almost level with the open door of the Bogles' bedroom, I heard a small explosion, and thinking that Victor was probably taking potshots at the bobbles on the lampshade, looked in to see. The room, a big one which opened onto a side veranda, was a crazy mixture of elegance and neglect. On one wall was a framed photograph of Faith's mother in the dress she'd worn for presentation at Government House. She had ostrich feathers in her hair, and her neck and one of her nostrils had been eaten away by silverfish. For the rest of it, there was a handsome old Turkoman carpet, a dead cumquat tree in a pot, bowls of fresh flowers on furniture which hadn't been dusted for weeks and in the middle of it all a big brass bed with enamelled inlays. Victor, in short pyjamas, was standing beside the bed with a bottle of champagne in his hand and Faith, a glass in hers, was lying propped against embroidered pillows. The Bogles always used embroidered bed linen and Faith changed it every day. It was her one extravagance. She had cupboards of handmade sheets and pillowslips, some of them still unused. She told me once that in the days when she was the pianist with a theatre orchestra, she'd spent half her salary on embroidered linen, having it made by a distant cousin of hers, a crippled girl, who lived somewhere in the hills behind Brereton.

That morning when Victor saw me standing in the doorway, he shouted, "Vinnie. Come in and celebrate. We're going to have a son."

Not certain if he was having one of his jokes, I hesitated and Faith, speaking so softly I hardly heard her, said, "It's true, Vinnie. I'm going to have a baby."

"A son," repeated Victor.

The word "baby" was the one that reached me. My God, I thought. They must be mad, and still in the doorway asked Faith if she was pleased.

Victor answered for her. "Of course she is. She thinks it's super. We're going to call him Rolfe after my grandfather. Here . . . " He'd filled Faith's glass and was holding another one out to me.

I went into the room and took it, and wanting to stare at Faith but not letting myself, stared instead at the dead cumquat tree.

Victor, who'd filled an empty teacup with champagne, raised it. "To Rolfe," he said.

I tried to repeat the words but embarrassment or something stopped me. Without toasting the baby, I gulped some wine and then I said, "What if it's a girl?"

"No chance! This time I'll get what I want." Victor drained the cup, beamed at me and left the room.

I let myself look at Faith then. She was as beautiful as ever, stunning really because her disordered hair and the champagne glass gave her a slightly wanton look. At the same time the morning light was strong enough to remind me that she was past forty and I asked myself how the hell she expected to get through a pregnancy and run the hotel as well.

She guessed I'm sure what I was thinking because still speaking softly, she said, "We'll muddle through, Vinnie, and I *am* pleased. The thought of having a son means the earth to Victor, so I'm pleased too."

She certainly looked it. To be honest, at that moment I felt a stab of jealousy towards her. She had a husband, four daughters, embroidered sheets and now a fetus inside her as well. What would she think, I asked myself, if she knew I had a child of my own — one who'd more or less disowned me? Squashing the thought, I went to Faith and kissed the top of her head. Then in a voice which was anything but hearty, I said, "I think you're crazy. But go on being happy."

"You won't leave me, will you, Vinnie? You're my brick, my rock, my tower of strength." She gave me her drowning look but I resisted it and said slowly, "Faith, you know I won't always be here."

"Nonsense," said Victor, coming in the door with a

tray of chicken pieces and bread and butter. "Of course you will. You're part of the family. Besides, you wouldn't leave the kids. They dote on you and you dote on them."

His words made me look into the future. I saw myself twenty years on — sitting on the veranda with my knitting, pleased because someone else's child had remembered my birthday. God no! Not me, I thought and knew that unless I was a fool, I should make plans before too long to leave The Bananas.

Victor put the tray on the bed and noticing that he'd decorated it with poinsettia blooms I asked him why he hadn't used a potted palm instead.

The joke delighted him. "You've seen them," he said and poured himself more champagne.

"Seen them? I've tried to *count* them. There must be a thousand."

"Eighteen hundred. The boys and I put them there last night when you were asleep."

Victor watched my face. I knew he was hoping to see me quail at the thought of men moving to and fro before my open door while I slept. His little exercise in terrorism was wasted. The palms had been put where they were in the evening when I was working in the kitchen; I knew that as surely as if I'd been there because if Victor and his cronies had been flitting around in the garden late at night, Billie would have raised the roof.

I stared back at Victor until he looked away and then I asked him where the palms had come from.

"I got them from Essen at the nursery," he said. "He let me have them for a song. His hired hand had left and he knew he wouldn't have time to repot them himself. I'll spend the winter doing it, a few a day and in the end I'll make a fortune. They sell for twenty dollars down the coast. Multiply that by eighteen hundred and you'll see what I mean."

167

I knew Victor wouldn't repot the trees, let alone get around to selling them. At the most he might do half a dozen, then he'd lose interest and the rest of the palms would sit, unwatered, in the garden till Kingdom Come. But he went on talking about them for some time and Faith, listening to him, smiled for all the world as if he'd pulled off a coup on the international money market.

To bring them back to earth, I asked Faith when she intended giving up her job at the school.

Again Victor answered for her. "We've talked about that and decided she can stay at work until she's five or six months. That'll take us to September and by then we'll have made a killing on the palms."

"And if you don't make a killing?"

"There speaks the old Tax Grouch," said Victor and after that I held my tongue.

Two days later, Mr Dunne, the hotel's only permanent guest, left to live with a widowed sister. As soon as his rooms had been cleaned, Faith advertised them in the local paper. They were taken by Marcia Scott, the twenty-six-year-old daughter of Faith's cousin, the one who'd done the needlework for her years before. During a gossipy reunion on the phone, Muriel Scott told Faith that Marcia, currently driving a taxi for someone on the coast, had been doing her Master's in Psychology but dropped out because she couldn't come to terms with the male hierarchy.

She arrived at The Bananas the next day when I was out. According to Faith, she parked the cab in the middle of the drive and flew up the steps with some yellow silk tulips in one hand and a bottle of vitamin B complex in the other. She took a quick look at the vacant rooms, put the tulips and the vitamins on the bed and vanished, coming back later in the day with the cab packed almost to the roof with records, books and clothes.

"You'll love her," Faith told me when I got home. "She's very much the liberated woman — cotton vest, no bra and a pair of knee-length khaki shorts. She made Victor's eyes bulge, I can tell you, but she seemed unmoved by the fact."

On meeting Marcia, I decided she could afford to be unmoved by most things. She was tall with a gymnast's body and the grace as well. Glossy sun-streaked hair worn skewered on top of her head in a loose doughnut shape heightened the Olympian image. She had the slight frown that short-sighted people sometimes wear and on her neck was a birthmark like a tiny string of coral islands. Her mouth was well shaped, her teeth good, but when you saw her eyes, you saw nothing else. They were long and wide and a stunning shade of silvery blue. Altogether, Marcia Scott was a tall strong beautiful woman and I could see that she knew it.

I saw little of her during her first weeks at the hotel. She worked the afternoon and evening shift with her cab and consequently slept late. When she did surface, she'd spend an hour on the side veranda stretching herself into advanced yoga postures, then after fruit and coffee in the kitchen she'd disappear. Behind her back, Victor and the claque made endless sex-related jokes about her; to her face they were courtly but careful to keep their distance. As for me, I was intrigued by Marcia and wanted to know more about her but didn't get the opportunity until the night Faith took me to a music recital in the rainforest in the hills behind The Estuary.

When Faith asked me to go with her, I'd accepted thinking the trip there in the Mini would give me a chance to point out that it was time for her to start thinking about getting help in the kitchen. I'd primed myself to throw in some grisly warnings about women of her age miscarrying but Faith didn't let me. Each time I broached the subject of the workload at the hotel, she turned the conversation so firmly into other channels that I knew I was being told to mind my own business and gave up.

The house where the recital was held crouched beneath soaring trees linked by ropes of creeper. It was built from materials salvaged from demolition sites and consisted of one large room with a mezzanine floor above it furnished with a bed and a bentwood chair. Most of the guests sat downstairs to listen to the music but a few dangled their legs from the bedroom.

The only light in the house came from a kerosene lamp and the musicians, two gentlemanly guitarists and a pale little cellist in a hand-knitted dress, spent as much of their time scrabbling for the right sheet of music as they did in playing. When they got going though they were damned good and that night as the stringed sounds of Bach floated through the house and the forest around it, I let myself forget the disquiet I was beginning to feel about living with the Bogles.

After the recital, the women present served supper of carrot cake and coffee made from some sort of grain. Faith, who seldom left The Estuary, enjoyed herself so much she stayed talking to Max, the host, until everyone else had gone and when at last we went out to the Mini, we found it wouldn't start.

Wearing borrowed sweaters against the cold, we tried for half an hour to get it going. In the end, Max, who had no car of his own, decided the starter motor had given up the ghost and set off by torchlight to find a neighbour with a telephone. Faith and I waited for him in the house and tried not to notice the eerie silence around us. In due course Max came back to say that Victor was coming to pick us up. But it turned out that the thought of having a taxi on call had been too much for the owner of The Bananas and it was Marcia not Victor who came for us.

The ride home was an extraordinary one. We shot downhill at a breathless pace while Faith and Marcia carried on a conversation about famous conductors. The road was a narrow one which snaked around bends so steep that on my side of the car, the forest fell away to nothing. The other two didn't seem to care if we were on the road or not and more than once we toured around the shoulder so that I longed to close my eyes but didn't dare. By the time we'd reached the coast road, and were sweeping along beside the moon-shot sea, they were discussing Beethoven's last quartet and I'm sure the pair of them would have driven on to Brisbane if I hadn't told them we were at The Estuary and the hotel just a little way ahead.

While I was getting out of the car, I heard Faith say, "Come inside and I'll get Victor to pay you."

Marcia said, "There's no charge but I think I've scared Vinnie half to death. I'm taking her to my room for a drink."

"Vinnie's had a long day." Faith's voice had a touch of sharpness. "I'm sure she's ready for bed."

By then Marcia had joined me at the side of the taxi. Taking my elbow, she said, "Let her off the hook, cousin," and steered me away.

I *was* tired but I went with Marcia through the splashy shadows of the garden and up onto the veranda. Outside her door we paused to admire the moon couched in the arms of a poinciana tree, then we stepped into the tiny room which opened into Marcia's bedroom. I saw the silk tulips in a jug on the table and caught my breath because above them on the wall was a drawing of my mother's head in profile. Almost immediately I realised it was Virginia Woolf, not Irene, but taken aback by that

171

first impression, I went on staring until behind me Marcia said, "Wasn't she exquisite?"

"Indeed she was, but for a moment, you know, I thought it was my mother."

"Were they alike?"

"Not terribly, but there's something — the nose, I think, and the angle of the head on that long neck." I turned to Marcia who was at the bookcase filling glasses. "My mother's looks were much admired. Especially by me. I longed and longed to look like her."

"Were you close?" Her face serious, concerned, she came across the room and handed me a drink. I smelt blackcurrant in it and something else.

"God no." I settled myself in a cane chair. "Nothing could be further from the truth. As a child I found Irene cold and distant. At eighteen I more or less ran away and we didn't meet for years."

Looking down into my drink I thought of the night I flew to Brisbane for my father's funeral. I wasn't expected till the next day and with no one to meet me, took a taxi from the airport. It was raining like fury.

At my parents' house I ran up the drive, left my squelching shoes on the veranda and let myself inside. The only light was a dim one coming from Irene's bedroom.

"Is that you Bart?" she called.

Without answering I went to her room. She was lying on the quilted cover of her bed and when she saw me, sat up to peer at me with anxious eyes. Then her face lightened. "Vinnie? My little girl." She stretched out her arms. "My sweet one."

The words undid me and in tears I went to her and knelt and put my face against hers. Holding me, Irene cried too and kept calling me her little girl.

We were together no more than five minutes when

172

Bart arrived. He had some papers for Irene to sign and after putting on another light brought them to the bed. I stood to let him get next to Irene. He stayed there and soon I went to the other side of the bed so that I could see her too. The next thing, Bart had followed me and was standing between us again. It seemed he had a lot of business to discuss and in the end, feeling I had no part in it, I wandered away to unpack and put on something dry.

Marcia, who'd returned to the bookcase and was sitting cross-legged in front of it, jogged me into the present by saying, "When you and your mother finally met, did you get along?"

"Yes and no. It was difficult because my brother was always there. He loved Irene more than I did. I was aware of that and aware of having run off. It made me feel awkward somehow and because of that I didn't push myself forward. Now, I think my mother was probably hurt by my seeming indifference."

"How do you know your brother loved her more?"

"He did — that's all."

"Are you sure he wasn't just protecting a good investment?"

Remembering Bart's conversation on the day of Irene's funeral and his attempt to charm me with the *Space Odyssey* music, I smiled a bit. "That's one way of looking at it," I said. "But to get back to Irene — after Dad died I visited her more or less regularly. I still didn't make an effort with her though, and now of course I wish I had." I paused to try my drink and decided the second ingredient was ouzo. "I tell myself that those years were reasonably happy ones for her, but I don't know that it's true."

"It probably is. Most women blossom when freed from the constraints of marriage."

173

"A lot do. But it's a complex issue because a lot fly back into the cage."

"More fool them." Putting her head on one side, Marcia studied my face. "I suppose you were your father's girl."

"Very much so. I can look back and see myself basking in his compliments and shrieking at his jokes in a way which must have been offensive to Irene."

"You can't blame yourself for that."

"I'm not so sure, because naive and all as I was, I've no doubt that in the bottom of my black little heart I saw myself as my mother's rival."

"Come off it — you're falling for the old Freudian bilge."

"Perhaps I am, but I'm also trying to be honest."

"Nonsense. I'll bet your father used the divide-and-rule manoeuvre with great skill and to top it off your brother observed it all and learned to do the same."

"Yes, but the point is that Irene and I let them get away with it and may have done so with the worst possible motives."

Marcia was silent, using the time I knew to choose a line of argument. Without giving her time to do so, I took a gulp of ouzo and said, "Y'know, I think the time's come when we should call a truce to all this sexual warfare and try to find out what causes it — what's *behind* it."

I'd finished my little speech rather lamely because halfway through it, Marcia, listening intently, had taken the pins from her hair. It fell to make a gleaming tent around her. Then, still listening, she gathered it in her hands, twisted it into a rope and fastened it deftly on top of her head again. While I was still off-balance from watching this conjuring trick, she said, "We already know that."

174

"We *do?*"

"Envy of the womb. That's what's behind it."

Aware of the ouzo surging in me. I said, "So tell me what the solution is."

"To remove ourselves from the bastards, of course. To leave them to show off to each other with their filthy bombs and rockets and make a sane world of our own."

"In a word — apartheid?"

"Yes, why not?"

Grinning, I said, "Because it wouldn't work. Our hormones would betray us."

"Mine wouldn't."

"Then you're lucky — I know mine would." I held out my empty glass.

While Marcia poured me another drink, I did a long-range scan of the bookcase. All the feminists were there from Wollstonecraft to Walker. I saw piles of journals on both female psychology and physiology and when Marcia handed me my drink and returned to sit with so much ammunition at her back, I wanted to grin again.

"Where were we?" she asked.

I took a long swallow of my drink and said, "I was getting ready to tell you about my belief that women are preoccupied with men while they scarcely know we exist."

"Bullshit! They know we exist all right and won't be satisfied until we *don't.*" Marcia shouted the words so fiercely that we both burst out laughing. That laughter, which went on and on, was some sort of watershed in our relationship because after it, I felt that we were friends.

When we'd simmered down, Marcia asked what had happened to my mother. I told her and she said, "I'm sorry. Your husband died too, didn't he?"

"Yes."

"Faith says you never speak of him."

Marcia, ready to weigh my answer, watched me closely, but I'd had enough soul baring for one night and dodged the issue by adopting a cockney accent and saying, "I'm trying to put the past behind me, luv."

For a second or two her silver eyes went on watching me, then she said, "Fair enough," and got up to take my empty glass again. As she did four members of the claque stormed the front steps. They'd been out to dinner somewhere and wore party hats. Seeing the light in Marcia's room, they stopped to peer at us. One, wearing a hat like a rooster's comb, let out a crow of laughter. The man behind gave him a push and they all charged into the hotel and out of sight.

"Bogle's gorillas," said Marcia. "Incidentally, what do you think of Victor?"

"I try not to."

"He's mad about you. You know that don't you?"

"*That's* bullshit. He can't stand me — I represent everything he disapproves of."

"That's why he's mad about you."

"According to that theory he'll be even worse about you."

Looking down at me, Marcia shook her head slowly from side to side. "Not at all. I don't have your vulnerability and it's the vulnerability that appeals to Victor."

"I'm far from vulnerable where he's concerned."

"But not where much else is, and that reminds me, you have to be up early slaving for Faith. I've been selfish keeping you." She extended a hand and I let her pull me to my feet.

We stood for a moment, our faces close, then Marcia whispered, "What is it you're hiding from, Vinnie Beaumont?"

"Myself, of course," I said and kissed her smooth cheek and fled.

From then on I saw a lot of Marcia. She started leaving work earlier at night and coming through the garden to see if I was still awake. If I was, she'd sit propped in the open doorway and entertain me with stories of the passengers she'd ferried up and down the coast that day.

"I'm building up your repertoire of stories," she'd say and launch into a description of a nineteen-year-old surf-lifesaver who had leukemia or the trawler skipper who'd cried when he learned his wife was working in a massage parlour.

Needless to say, a lot of Marcia's male passengers made passes at her. I asked her once if that worried her. Her reply was cool and easy. "I'm stronger than most of them and certainly fitter. They don't bother me at all."

Not once in that period did we return to the dialogue of sexual politics nor did Marcia question me again about my past. But one night, to my surprise, I began to talk about it myself. Marcia was lounging in the armchair, I sat on the edge of the table with the cat stretched beside me, and Billie at my feet. We'd been driven from the doorway by a shower of rain which hammered madly on the roof for three or four minutes then stopped.

"It rained like that," I said, "after I took Brook's ashes to the forest and scattered them around."

Marcia didn't move an eyelash.

"I took them there because I thought it was where he'd want to be. Then I went home believing that in some sort of fashion I could go about the business of my life. But when I lay in bed that night, the rain came and it undid me. Y'know, you don't get ashes from the crematorium at all. You get little pieces of bone and I couldn't bear to think of those little pieces of Brook lying in the

177

rain. I guess I was out of my mind because at first light I drove back to the forest and picked them up again. It took me hours to find them and when I was satisfied I had them all, I put them in a cedar jewel box Brook had made for me, then I climbed the fence of the old goldmine cemetery at Gillie. There, with only Billie and the graves of people dead a hundred years for company, I buried them."

All the time I was speaking, I kept my eyes fastened on a plaited cotton rug on the floor. Keeping them there, I said, "I went home thinking again that I could go about the business of my life." I shot a look at Marcia. "But I couldn't, because I wasn't able to forgive Brook for leaving me." A long pause. "That's childish, isn't it?"

"Not at all. Bitterness is very much a part of grief — people don't realise it, that's all."

My eyes back on the rug, I said, "When he was alive, Brook used to tell me a Zen story about some wild geese. The point of it was that once you've had an experience, nothing can take it away from you. When I finally saw that, it allowed me to come to terms with the fact that he'd gone, but I still *blamed* him for it, and you see, the reason I didn't talk about him was because I was afraid that if I tried, I'd open my mouth and scream and scream." I raised my hands. "Suddenly speaking of him seems the natural thing to do."

"Which means you've finally put the bitterness behind you."

"Yes, I have and the funny thing is that another man's departure helped me do it." I looked back at Marcia. "Soon after I came to The Bananas, I met a man I liked. I mean, really liked. He went away too and in the sadness that came after, I saw the difference between someone who leaves voluntarily and someone who has no

178

choice. I feel that's the *real* meaning of the story about the wild geese and I'm just surprised it took so long to work it out."

Marcia and I stared at each other and in the quietness of the room I could hear Billie's breathing. "You know I've never told this stuff to anyone, not even . . ." I was going to say, "my daughter," but changed it to "my friend Hannibal."

"I'm glad I was the one you chose to tell." Marcia stood and came across the room to put her arms around me. I stayed in her embrace, breathing a perfume which reminded me again of my mother — rose, I think it was, with a trace of something sharper like verbena. I felt relaxed and comforted, yet there was a tiny corner of my consciousness which wondered why I'd been unable to mention the grief I *hadn't* put behind me. The grief of losing Clare.

15

On an evening softened by a big persimmon moon, I let Marcia make love to me in the rough grass which bordered the beach. We'd been walking and had sat beside the beach to talk. Before long we were on the subject of the Bogles. Marcia, labelling Victor sexist-of-the-century, said that it was our job to rescue Faith.

"I used to feel that way," I told her, "but I've realised that's the last thing she wants. Being a martyr is Faith's idea of heaven."

"Yes, because she's been indoctrinated." Marcia gestured impatiently, "It's up to us to undo the damage." She turned to look at me. "You're close to her. Talk to her, tell her what a fool she is."

"I tried that but she didn't want to know and since then I've come to the conclusion that only a fool interferes in other people's marriage games."

"Then *I* must find a way to punish Victor."

Marcia's vehemence made me laugh. Then I lay back in the grass, looked up at the showy red moon and hearing the little lap of water on the shore, told myself to forget the Bogles and enjoy the night. The next moment, Marcia's face appeared above me, it grew big and blotted out the moon. Then she kissed me.

I received the kiss in the giggly manner of a twelve-year-old but as she kissed me again I found that her softness and the long-familiar perfume she wore combined to manufacture a charm of their own. I stayed there as shameless and receptive as a sea anemone while she set about showing her expertise at lesbian lovemaking. Her surprisingly strong tongue and cunning fingers understood exactly the responses of my mouth and breasts and of the folded flower inside the lips of my vagina. Before long I ceased to be myself at all and became instead the pulse at the centre of the universe, the moan. But later, spent and reflective, I realised that for me the experience had lacked something because I'd missed the *completing* that only penetration gives; had missed too the sweet little time of truce that follows it. That knowledge was the second secret I kept from Marcia and I suppose the second betrayal.

Two days after the sex scene at the beach, Faith found some spots of blood on her underpants. She was at school when it happened, and aghast at the thought of losing Victor's son, rushed home and asked me in a whisper what to do.

"Ring your doctor straightaway," I said and when Faith did so, she was told to go to bed and stay there for at least three weeks. Pausing only long enough to tell Victor she'd come home with a virus, she went to her room and began undressing.

That night I bathed the children and gave them their tea early. Then, to give myself a breather before starting the dinner, I took a drink in to Faith. She was propped against her embroidered pillows and had on the glasses she hardly ever wore.

As I entered the bedroom, she stretched an arm towards me and said, "You won't give me away to Victor, will you?"

I tried to make my voice tough, "If you don't get some help in the kitchen, I will."

181

Certain of me, she smiled, but as she did the light catching her glasses, blanked out her eyes and turned her face into one I didn't know.

Still smiling, she held up the knitting she'd been doing. It was a baby's jacket, bunched where Faith had made a mistake in the pattern and grubby from travelling backwards and forwards to school in her music case.

My God, I thought, who knitted the last lot? And making an excuse about getting back to the children, I left her.

In the hall I met Marcia who came flying around the corner from the direction of the office. Seeing me, she stopped, frowned in her short-sighted way and said, "I've been looking for you."

Out of sorts from my visit to Faith, I chose that moment to ask how she'd managed to pass the sight test for a taxi licence.

Marcia ignored the question. Putting her hands up to tighten her topknot, she came close to me. "I need to talk to you," she said. "I picked up two kids today walking up the coast road — a girl of twelve hauling a suitcase and a boy of eight lagging behind with blistered heels."

"Where are they now?"

"That's it — I don't know. I lost them."

Just then Chris Tilley and Don Leembruggen, both in boardshorts, came through the billiard room and into the hall. Don was carrying a tennis ball. I saw him say something to Chris, then he dodged past us and lobbed the ball over our heads. Chris caught it and lobbed it back. The next moment it whizzed by at head height, unpleasantly close and going fast.

"Ignore them," said Marcia, but when the ball flew by again she shot out an arm and caught it neatly. Turning to Chris, she said, "If I give it back, will you go away?"

Grinning, he said, "What about a foursome?"

"Just piss off." Marcia threw him the ball. He lobbed it slowly over our heads, then ducked past us and he and Don went along the hall and turned out of sight.

"Cretins," said Marcia. "Anyway, where was I?"

"About the kids. Go back to the beginning."

"Right." She paused to collect her thoughts. "I picked them up, as I said, on the coast road about four. At first the girl didn't want to get in the cab but her brother's blisters won the day. I asked where they were going and the girl — Penny, she called herself — was cagey enough to say, 'Up north', and no more. But I did learn that they'd come all the way from Melbourne and been on the run for six weeks. They were down at Surfers most of the time. One week was spent in a patch of trees beside the Nerang River. After that they lived in an empty highrise building."

"What did they do for food and stuff?"

"Apparently they'd started out with quite a bit of cash. When it was gone the girl shoplifted from supermarkets and fruit stalls. She told me that for the whole time they were at Surfers, she sent her brother to school each day. Not only that, but sent him with his clothes washed and his homework done. I must have looked disbelieving at that piece of information because she opened the suitcase and on top of clothes and things there were his bloody school books."

"Did she tell you why they left home?"

"She said that her father, a schoolteacher if you please, beat her, but something on her face when she said it, made me think he did more to her than beat her."

I thought that over and asked where she'd let them out.

"I didn't. That's the point. I took them to the cafe at Inkey's Inlet for a meal and while they were having it, I told them I'd take them up to Mum's. That they could stay there as long as they liked if they did a few chores for her. At first Penny was delighted but she must've thought it over and decided the offer was too good to be true because later, when I stopped to deliver a parcel at the bait factory, the two of them disappeared. I spent an hour going up and down the road looking for them. I even went along the beach but they'd vanished as if they'd never been."

"Did you go to the police?"

"Of course I didn't. Do you think I'm mad? If *they* find Penny, she'll be sent straight home to Dad."

"Come off it — those days are in the past. Besides, Todd West, the copper here, is a decent bloke with kids of his own."

Marcia thrust her face close to mine so that hers was suddenly big and plain. "I know all about decent men and their daughters. I've had first-hand experience." She grabbed my arm. "Listen Vinnie — I want you to go down to the jetty and ask the Dead End Kids if they've seen those two children and if they haven't, to keep an eye out for them. You can bet that lot's got some sort of underground going."

"If they knew anything, they wouldn't tell."

"They might tell *you*. It's a worth a try."

"I couldn't go till after dinner."

"But you will?"

"Yes, if you want me to, but I still think you should go to the police."

"Let's try the kids on the jetty first." Marcia beamed, then hugged me. "Love you Vinnie," she said as Victor came around the corner and stopped to stare at us.

Marcia let go of me and without looking at Victor, hurried towards the outside door. I stayed where I was and gave the host of The Bananas back his glassy stare until he too turned away.

The moon was fat and friendly that night when I went to see the Dead End Kids, but there was nothing friendly about the place where they lived. Perched at the end of the jetty, it was a dilapidated building which had once been a picture theatre. At high tide the water was only inches below its slatted floor and for some of the time at least, the possessions of those inside must have been wet. During the summer storm we'd had, the entrance and box office blew into the estuary. Later, the kids had salvaged what they could and patched up the damage but part of the wall was still missing and the space had been filled with an Indian quilt which rose and fell in the wind. Above it was the remains of a poster advertising *Mary Poppins* with part of King Kong's body showing through.

That night as I trod my way towards the picture theatre, I saw the jetty had been newly decorated with six potted palms standing in pairs at intervals of ten feet or so. They looked as raffish as all get-out, and perhaps because I knew where they'd come from, somehow sad as well.

There was no light in the theatre but when I'd passed the first pair of palms, I heard music. It was panpipe music, a lonely sound which fitted in only too well with everything around me. At the second pair of palms, I smelled marijuana and a little further on I saw the quilt move. A head came out, looked and disappeared again. I stopped and waited. Suddenly the quilt was pushed aside. A young man came out; he walked into the moonlight and stood there. It was Gary, the boy whose jacket had offended Victor so much.

"It's Vinnie Beaumont," I sang out. "I want to talk to you."

The music stopped. I heard a baby cry then that stopped too.

Gary didn't answer me and I called, "I'm looking for a little girl."

Still no answer.

"She was with her brother. A friend of mine picked them up today and brought them as far as The Estuary."

Gary's only response was to shift his head a little and the moonlight glinted on an earring.

Desperate because I knew I was making a hash of things, I blurted, "They're on the run and they need help."

Instead of answering he turned, walked back and had a whispered conversation with someone on the other side of the quilt. Another wave of marijuana reached me. Then Gary came back to where he'd been before. "How old's the girl?" he said.

"Only twelve."

He was silent again, so I said, "Her name's Penny and you know, don't you, what'll happen to her if someone doesn't help?"

"I've got a good idea."

"So have you seem them?"

Whoever it was at the quilt popped out, spoke briefly to Gary and vanished.

"We haven't seen the kid," said Gary. "Or her brother."

I was stymied. For all I knew Penny was behind the quilt listening to me, and if she was, there wasn't a hope in hell of my finding out.

I was about to turn away when Gary stopped me by saying, "What's it to you, anyway?"

"Oh, come on. She's a nice little girl. Believe it or not, I was like that once."

He seemed to relax a little. There was another silence and I heard the water lapping beneath me. Then in a friendlier tone, Gary said, "They aren't here, if that's what you think. But we'll keep a lookout for them."

"And let us know?"

"Maybe."

Inside the theatre the baby began to cry again. I went a few steps towards Gary and lowering my voice a little said, "If Victor Bogle sees the palms, he'll go to the police. He's dying for the opportunity."

"The cops won't give a fuck." Gary began to mimic my voice, "If Victor wants his palms, he'll have to come and get them." After that he waited until I was halfway to the shore and called out, "What's it like, Missus Beaumont, living up there with all those dudes?"

"It has its moments," I shouted back.

"When you feel like some of the real thing come down and let me know."

He was being as cheeky as he knew how; at the same time he was letting me know I'd passed some sort of test.

Without turning I waved a hand in the air and went back to The Bananas.

Later that night I learned from Loretta Burns that Penny and her brother had already been picked up by the police and were safely tucked into bed at Todd West's place. Later again Marcia rang with the same news. For us that was more or less the end of the matter, though I knew the image of the little girl with the suitcase and the boy with the blistered heels would haunt both of us for a long time to come.

Marcia called at my room that night while I slept. She left a note saying she'd been hired to drive a marine biologist as far as Rockhampton and would be away for a week. The note was signed with a drawing of a faceless person seated in the lotus position.

That little drawing of Marcia's worried me. Perhaps I read too much into it, but I felt its facelessness was an indication of the fact that Marcia was aware I hadn't committed myself to her in the way she'd committed herself to me. I had the feeling too that when she came back she'd press me for a clarification of the terms of our relationship.

Knowing I wouldn't be able to give her the answers she'd be hoping for, I stood looking into the morning garden and asked myself what it was I wanted from life. I stayed there, peeling away onion skins of half-truth in my mind until I made myself admit I wanted most of all to have a cheerful and loving reunion with my daughter, wanted too a man, as tolerant and charming as Brook had been, to come riding out of the west and tie up at my door.

Then deciding that I'd plumped for impossibilities, I asked myself what I'd settle for instead. More peeling away of half-truths resulted in the answer: modest success someday with my stories, and to have a continuing friendship with Marcia as long as it stopped short of full commitment.

Two more impossibilities, I thought, and neither of them enough to fill a lifetime. Then, with the problem still unsolved, I went to have my shower.

That afternoon, Victor spotted the palms on the jetty. Practically frothing at the mouth, he came home and after tossing down a rum bracer, rushed to the police station.

Todd West heard him out, then asked him if he could prove the palms were his and while Victor was still boggling at him, asked if he knew how many unemployed people there were in the country. Unable to see the connection between the two questions, Victor tried to stare him out. West, stolid and sure of himself, stared back until Victor turned and flew from the building.

He spent the next two days contacting senior police officials and members of parliament in an effort to have something done about what he called Constable West's dereliction of duty. On all sides he was given assurances of help but no one did anything and the palms went on waving their fronds in front of the old picture theatre. In the end, Victor appealed to the claque by asking some of its members to take their rugby muscles down to the jetty and repossess the potplants. To his horror, they refused.

One of them said, "Come on, Victor, a joke's a joke, and let's face it, the Dead End Kids pulled a good one."

Don Leembruggen chimed in, "Hell and Tommy, we can't pick on that lot. Not the thing, Skip, not the thing at all."

Slowly, Victor's eyes travelled around the circle of their faces and back again. No doubt he thought his will was strong enough to carry the day, but no one budged and in the end Victor returned defeated to the grog cupboard in the bathroom. That night he drank himself insensible and spent the next twenty-four hours in bed, while Faith, who was supposed to be in bed herself, fussed over him and mixed him hangover cures.

When he finally reappeared, Victor let go with a volley of remarks about the amount of guts and fire *his* son would have, then taking the thermos of coffee Faith had made him, he went to the garage and set about putting the finishing touches to his Jaguar. He must have felt like death itself but in spite of that, he worked late into the night, and the next day had the car on the road.

For the rest of the week, Victor was seldom out of the Jag. Wearing a cream motoring cap, he'd leave the hotel soon after breakfast and return in the evening. More than once seeing his excited face as he hurried out to the garage, I was reminded of certain parts of *The Wind in the Willows*.

On Saturday, Faith went with him and in the afternoon, with no one else available for parent-duty, I took Jami and Peta to a birthday party. At teatime Peta overate and half an hour after we got home was complaining of stomach pains. The Bogles were still away but Faith's friend Loretta Burns had arrived to weekend with an American major attached to the army hospital back in the bush. Catching her as she left their room, I asked her to look at the child for me.

Alight with love and preoccupied as well, Loretta prodded at Peta's abdomen and felt her forehead. "This little piggy had too much party." She said, "Just keep her quiet and she'll be okay." Heading for the door, she called back, "I must fly. Al and I are going to a bash on someone's yacht."

At nine, Peta started vomiting. Holding her head as she sweated and strained over a basin, I was suddenly swept by the need to see and hold my own daughter. The need had come without warning and was so strong it caused a part-pain, part constriction in my chest. I did my best to overcome it and concentrate on Peta but later, when I took her soiled sheets and pyjamas outside, the feeling was still with me.

As I crossed the backyard a car, flying in the side gate, pinned me with its lights. It stopped a few feet from me. I turned my head away and waited for the Bogles to emerge from the dazzle. But it was Marcia, with her straight back and easy stride, who came to me. She was wearing white, white shirt, white jeans. Her hair was looped at one shoulder in a thick plait with starry little jasmine flowers in it.

"I've had a wonderful trip," she said and hugged me. "But Vinnie, I missed you just too much."

Her joy, even the manner of her arrival, seemed an intrusion upon my mood of misery and the only greeting I managed to give her was an almost soundless "Hallo."

Still holding me, Marcia asked what was wrong.

"Just tired, I guess."

Her answer was to grab the bed-linen from my arms and run with it to the garage where she shoved it somewhere out of sight.

Back with me again, she said, "Go inside and put on your party gear. I'm taking you out. Two friends of mine, Josie and Barbara, drove down behind me. They're staying at the Inlet and I said I'd take you down to meet them."

"I'm sorry Marcia, I can't go with you. Peta's sick."

"Very sick?"

"Not really. She's been vomiting but she's asleep now."

"Then why can't you come?"

"Because no one else is home."

"What about Faith?"

"She's out. Victor got the Jag going and they've been out all day."

"I see. And what about Victor's little surfing friends, can't you ask one of them to play mother?"

"I suppose I could, but it doesn't seem fair."

Her face set and angry, Marcia stared at me. "Those bloody Bogles," she said and turned and went back to the taxi. She got in, switched off the lights and without looking at me again, started the engine. As she drove away, I saw her tugging at the collar of her shirt as if to make certain her birthmark was covered up.

I went inside understanding Marcia's anger but resenting it too. No doubt that's why I said "Yes" when Chris Tilley stuck his head out of the bathroom and asked me if I'd like him to mix me a zombie. After a second one, I told myself I was enjoying Chris's company as much as I enjoyed Marcia's and to be fair to him, when we went to the billiard room for a slapstick game of snooker, he made me laugh my ill-humour away so that by the time I went to bed I was relaxed enough to sleep.

I woke once during the night to hear Faith's voice somewhere in the hotel, and slept again to be woken by the sound of Billie's growling. It stopped almost immediately then Marcia squatted beside the bed. The jasmine was still in her hair but she'd swapped her shirt for a high-necked black skivvy with no sleeves and her face and arms made pale shapes in the gloom.

"Are you awake?" she whispered.

"Yes." For some reason I whispered too.

"Good, then I want you to get up and pack. We're leaving here tonight."

The words surprised a rough little laugh out of me. "Rather sudden, isn't it?"

Still whispering, she said, "I've got to get you away from here and it must be tonight."

I think the zombies were still with me because I crooned, "Up, up and away in my beautiful balloon."

"This isn't the time for jokes." Steadying herself with a hand on the floor, Marcia leaned towards me. "The girls and I stole Victor's Jaguar tonight."

Shocked by what she'd said, but not believing it, I sat up and tried to read her face.

"It's true. We took it over an hour ago."

"Then you'd better put it back."

"We can't. We drove it as far as the Toomey lookout and pushed it off into the sea."

"For Christ's sake." My voice was thin with dismay.

"I told you I'd find a way to even the score. Now do you see why we have to leave?"

I lay back against my pillow and said, "I don't know what to say to you."

"Don't say anything. Just get up and pack."

I didn't move. "The salt will ruin the car. It'll be worthless."

"So much the better."

I sat up again. "Are you silly enough to think you can achieve things by aping male aggression?"

"It's the way to defeat the bastards."

"The way to beat them is by teaching women to think for themselves."

"As you did with Faith?"

"Marcia, it's taken thousands of years to form society into its present pattern. We can't expect to change it overnight."

"Girl, the history books don't even *mention* us!"

"I know that, but I also know that in the last ten years we've made enormous strides. At least male historians are apologising for past omissions."

"That's not enough."

"Then I go back to my point about teaching women to think because I'm damned sure the inequalities of the past were made possible through their connivance."

Too angry to speak, Marcia stared at me as I went on. "There's a certain amount of truth in the old saying that the evil men do is known but the evil women do is done in secret."

Still staring at me, Marcia got to her feet. "Do you believe that?"

"Yes, I do."

"Then you'll be happy to stay here and play the lackey for the Bogles."

"No I won't. I mean to leave, but I'll stay till Faith finds someone to replace me."

"You'll wait a long time." Marcia turned away from me and moved into the centre of the room. There, I saw her unravel her hair and put the sprigs of jasmine on my table. At that stage I wasn't certain what to expect. I suppose I thought she'd come back to the bed and try to seduce me into her idea of reason. Instead she wound her hair up quickly, fastened it and without looking at me went to the door and disappeared.

For a few seconds I stayed where I was, thinking, she's gone, just like that! Then realising she had indeed, I leapt out of bed, grabbed my kimono and started to follow her. On the way I stumbled over Billie and by the time I'd reached the door, the little path through the palms was empty.

It was beginning to grow light and while I stood wondering what to do, a fruit-bat flapped across the garden on its strange homemade-looking wings. Then from the other side of the hotel I heard a car start and go quietly down the side street. At the corner it turned onto the highway and roared away to the south.

16

I went back to bed but instead of sleeping I lay awake smelling the little dying flowers on the table and mulling over the might-have-beens of my relationship with Marcia. I spent some time too grieving for the once faultless car. The knowledge that I might have forestalled the theft and all its implications if I'd gone with Marcia earlier in the night was a bitter pill for me to swallow.

Now and then I abandoned my misery to scold myself for not having handled better the last argument I'd had with her. I wanted to be left with the feeling that she'd gone away well and truly trounced by my logic. Why didn't I point out, I asked myself, that when they gave us the vote, they gave us everything? All we have to do is learn to use it.

So it went on until, long after daylight, I heard urgent steps and voices in the main hall. I got up then and still in my kimono, went to see what was happening. The first person I met was Faith who hurried towards me in Victor's dressing gown.

"The Jag's gone," she said, "Victor put it in the garage just after one and now it isn't there."

"How extraordinary." The words sounded false and inadequate but Faith was too agitated to notice.

"Come and see." Together we walked through the

hotel to the side door and looked across at the garage. In its heyday it'd been a tennis pavilion and on the side facing the court, instead of a wall there was a fancy arch of lattice. To see the place with little in it but the washing machine and a few faded streamers hanging from the light fitting made me feel as guilty as if I'd taken the car myself. In fact my face began to flush with guilt.

"By some miracle," said Faith, "we insured the wretched thing a month ago. Not that it matters, it's obvious the Dead End Kids took it and this time the police will have to do something."

"You can't be certain it was them."

Faith looked at me, saw my heightened colour and thinking no doubt it came from indignation, turned and went back inside. I followed her and in the hall, mumbling something about getting dressed, made my escape.

After checking on the children — both blooming, they were eating breakfast in the kitchen with Loretta — I went to Marcia's room. The door was shut and on opening it I saw that everything was gone, the books, the tulips, the drawing of Virginia Woolf. The only thing left behind in that sad little place was a shopping list with things like pecan nuts and toothpaste written on it. Till then I'd had some sort of childish notion that Marcia would reappear and manage to put things right. Realising that wasn't likely to happen I shut the door again and went to my own room where I more or less hid for the next hour. In the end, unable to concentrate on things like reading, I dressed and sought Loretta out again.

I found her on the side veranda where Marcia had done her yoga exercises. As casually as I could I asked for the latest news on the car theft.

"You wouldn't believe the carry on," Loretta said. "It's been ridiculous. Al stayed last night but this morning's performance from Victor sent him back to the base without breakfast."

"Tell me about it."

"Well, Constable West came to inspect the place and pointed out that a car housed in a tennis pavilion is asking to be taken. That didn't go down well with Victor, but I'd say that on the whole, he's enjoying the situation. He's the centre of attention and true to form loves every minute of it. Apart from that, a sergeant and a CIB man are on their way from Noosa or somewhere, so Victor's certain he'll soon have the Jag back and see the Dead End Kids thrown into gaol as well."

I filled in the rest of that awful morning by working in the kitchen. There were stacks of dishes to do and when I'd finished them I was kept busy making cups of coffee. It seemed that everyone at The Estuary had heard of the theft and during the course of the morning they dropped in one after the other to talk about it. What Loretta had told me about Victor turned out to be true. He *was* enjoying the situation. He'd installed himself in the bathroom and with a planter's punch in his hand regaled his buddies with stories of what he'd said to the police and of cars he'd owned in the past.

As for Faith, she seemed to be everywhere, one moment turning up in the kitchen to oversee the coffee making, the next standing in the bathroom doorway to listen to Victor. A little before twelve she announced that because of the crowd we'd serve a sit-down lunch and when I told her to forget the crowd and get off her feet, she looked at me as if I'd gone mad and began hauling food out of the fridge.

Suddenly I wanted more than anything to be away from The Bananas. While I made bowls of green salad, I kept thinking of Irene's house which was empty again. I thought of the quietness there and the way the sun slotted through the venetian blinds. Most of all, I thought of myself stretching out on the plump old couch and being able to sleep the clock around.

At lunch, Victor was in fine form. He told a lot of jokes and with encouragement from the claque made up a ditty about the defeat of the Dead End Kids. For me that ditty was the last straw. Hearing it, I knew that instead of waiting as I'd planned, I should leave immediately or else hear my voice telling the truth about the car and what had happened to it.

Not stopping for such things as second thoughts, I got to my feet as soon as the applause had finished and told Victor I'd like to see him alone for a few minutes.

He leered at me over his wine glass. "I'd like to see you alone too, doll."

Ignoring the laughter, I pressed on. "I'm serious Victor. I've something to tell you."

He was about to cap my remark but the look on my face stopped him and instead he stood up and came around the table.

"What is it?" he said.

"Not here. In private."

Eyes not leaving my face, he said, "All right. Come to the office."

As he'd done the day we met, he put his arm behind my back and together we left the room. On the way we passed Faith who swivelled a little in her chair to watch as we went by.

When we reached the office Victor ushered me in and pushed the door almost shut behind us.

"Victor, I . . . " That was as far as I got because he interrupted in a quick breathy voice, "I wasn't joking, doll, when I said I wanted to see you. I've been trying to see you alone for days. There's something here I want to show you." And going to the bookcase, he fumbled behind a row of books.

"Not now, Victor, it's important that we talk."

"This is important too." He flourished a parcel wrapped in tissue paper and tied with ribbon.

Watching my face again, he put it on the table. Impatiently, I pushed it back towards him. "Not now."

I don't think he heard me. He was so hot to show me what was in the parcel that he'd grabbed it again and was trying to undo the ribbon. When it wouldn't give, he swore under his breath and looked around for the evil-looking stiletto he used for opening letters. Finding it behind him on the bookcase, he seized it and cut through the ribbon.

"Please listen." I reached out and touched his arm but instead of stopping, Victor smiled at me and whipped the paper away from the parcel. "There, what do you think of that?" With a flourish, he rolled a necklace onto the table. I saw a row of creamy gumnuts interspersed with jade green leaves. Not my taste, but pretty just the same.

"It's charming," I told him. "Faith will love it."

He froze, giving me one of his mad stares, and I realised that the necklace wasn't meant for Faith at all; it was meant for me.

Unable to cope with this new and ridiculous subplot in my life I ignored it and rushed into a speech of resignation. "Victor, my mother's house is empty and I want to move to it." A shaft of inspiration reached me, "I'd like to concentrate on writing for a while and for that I need to be alone."

"Don't lie!" He spat the words. "You're going after your obscene friend."

I was too surprised to find an answer and he went on. "You thought I didn't know, but I've been watching you. I know the bitch came back yesterday. I even know that she and her filthy mates took my car."

199

Soundlessly my lips formed the word, "How?"

"Because the crazy creature rang me this morning. She's down in New South Wales and thinks she's safe. She rang to gloat."

She didn't need to do that, I thought and said aloud, "Have you told the police?"

"No, that'll keep. I'll see the scum moved off the jetty first. Then I'll tip the bucket on your friend."

I tried to speak but Victor didn't let me. "If you're planning to run after that freak, you'd better think again."

In a voice more tired than anything else, I said, "If Marcia's a freak, so are you."

He turned his head away briefly and said, "You bitch." He said it softly and as he did he lunged at me. I felt something sting the bridge of my nose and my cheek as well. Behind me I heard a funny noise and from the corner of my eye saw Faith, who'd pushed the door open. She was making the noise through her mouth as she breathed.

Victor was staring at me again, but his face had changed. It was as white as death and moving in slow motion, he put the stiletto he was holding down on the table.

I clamped my hand to my face and left them both, brushing past Faith who stopped making the noise long enough to say to me, "I don't want you near my children."

I got as far as the main hall. It seemed dark and a hundred miles long. At the end of it, there was a blaze of Queensland sun which started to move about. To stop it, I grabbed onto a chair and stayed there. Then someone took hold of my shoulders and held them until someone else, Loretta I think, prised my fingers away from my face and pushed a towel filled with ice against it.

200

Like that, with the towel against my face, I was led stumbling to a car and driven to the hospital. There, they sat me in a funny little room with a filing cabinet in it and a raincoat hanging on the door. I think I was alone for a while, then Loretta was bending over me.

"Old Doc Ramsay's on a fishing trip," she said, "but Al's coming in from the base."

I tried to ask her how bad my face was but my voice was so queer she couldn't understand me.

Before I could ask her again, she said, "Don't worry — Al's a fine surgeon," and putting her arm around me, she rested her head against mine.

While Loretta was still there, the sister on duty gave me an injection and that seemed to undo me because in a little while I began to cry. I was still crying when Al got there. He came in a helicopter, flying it himself and landing on the football field next door.

I don't remember walking anywhere but suddenly I was lying in another room and the towel was gone from my face. Al Sutton, with his freckles and his almost lashless eyes leaned over me.

"Well, Vinnie Beaumont, this sure is your lucky day." His Texan drawl was so thick it sounded phoney.

"No, it's not," I whispered.

He was looking all the time at the cut on my face. "Sure, it is. I was in Vietnam — you know that? I sewed hundreds of faces there. Thousands. I got to be mighty good at it — Suture Sutton, they called me, and Suture Sutton is gonna stitch your face so damned beautiful, no one will know it was cut."

Loretta's head floated into sight. "He means it," she said and vanished.

My face was cleaned with something that hurt, then Al Sutton was back again. "I'll shoot in some anesthetic," he told me, "and stitch you up with stuff like silk. Okay, now here we go."

201

The hypodermic in front of my eyes seemed as big as a cannon, so I closed them and kept them closed all the way through, but I can tell you this, it's no joke having your face sewn up. I think if it was your arm or something, you could look down at it and not care too much, but when someone sews your face, it's as if they were sewing into your soul.

Later, because she couldn't very well take me back to The Bananas, Loretta put me to bed at the hospital. She put me in an empty ward with two beds in it and a window overlooking the estuary. I lay there between glassy sheets and felt more alone than I'd been before in my life. I wanted to use my fingers to explore the sutures on my face but I'd been told not to, so I didn't. Once or twice I cried again but in the end I fell asleep.

Some time in the evening, I woke to find Loretta bending over me examining her lover's needlework.

"Perfect," she said. "You really are lucky, you know."

"From where I am, I don't feel too bloody lucky."

"Nonsense. Al says that in two years you'll only have a hairline mark."

I sat up in bed and wailed, "Two years. *Two years!* God Almighty, I'd rather be dead."

"Vinnie, be a little thankful. It could have been a lot worse. And think of Al. He'll be shot, y'know, for taking the helicopter."

There was a flurry of noise in the hall and I sat up in time to see someone being wheeled past on a trolley.

Loretta turned from me then and went to the bed next to mine. Although not a thing in that shiny little ward was out of place, she made a pretence of straightening the pillows. "That was Faith," she said. "She miscarried a little while ago and Victor brought her here. We've put her just along the corridor."

It was then that I began to laugh. I laughed like a

lunatic even though it hurt my face. In the end of course the laughter turned to tears and it seemed that nothing the hospital staff did for me could stop them.

17

It started to rain some time in the night and when I woke at three a.m. it was still raining. Instead of going to sleep again I lay with my eyes open and listened to it whispering on the roof. It had a malicious sound and reminded me of the way Miss Broome talked when I was at school. Miss Broome was the dread of the fourth form. She was a tall woman with upswept gunmetal hair and a handsome face. When she wished to be particularly scathing, she lowered her voice and made sibilant sounds as she spoke. I spent two years in fourth form and knew her well. That night in the little hospital at The Estuary, I used old Bully Broome as a starting point and ran a distinctly morbid little movie of my life through my mind, lingering long enough on the low spots to convince myself there was in me some sort of poison which finished off my relationships with other people. After that I wallowed in a sea of self-pity so deep it seems funny now to think of it, but at the time it was anything but funny. For the life of me I couldn't see how I'd fill in my future or even where I'd turn for friends. In the end I told myself to be like a reformed alcoholic and concentrate on getting through each twenty-four hour period as it came up. That idea encouraged me to the point of making plans to move my animals and things back to my mother's house.

The rain stopped at daylight and almost immediately some kind of dove outside began to call, "Coo-coll, Coo-coll." I got out of bed then and went to the window to look at the estuary. If I'd hoped to find solace by gazing into the eye of nature, I was bound for disappointment. In the early light, the sky and river were a washed-out grey and apart from a row of pelicans sitting with sagelike dignity on the sandbar, there was nothing to see. I stood at the window until some half-hearted colour showed above the horizon and as I went to turn away, I saw two people come around the corner of the hospital. Against a backdrop of dripping bushes, they left the path and cut across the lawn towards a gap in the side fence. Where they'd come from and where they were heading, I've no idea. In front was a man I'd seen hanging around the post office steps. He was about fifty and no more than five foot two, with the kind of grey hair which had once been ginger. A few paces behind was his twenty-year-old Filipino bride, who clutched an acrylic cardigan across her pregnant belly and wore Argyle socks with her sandals. The man didn't see me but the woman did. For a few seconds she stared at my mended face and hospital nightshirt. Then, without an atom of expression on her face she moved on.

Dear God, I thought, she's past feeling sympathy or hope or even amusement, and suddenly I was appalled by the memory of the harsh things I'd said to Marcia the night before. Why didn't I turn the coin over? I asked myself. Why didn't I remember that women are the strong and humorous ones, the creative ones; that behind almost every creative man there's a woman feeding him ideas?

The couple reached the fence, climbed through and disappeared, but I stayed at the window until I'd worked out that as a starting point in my seemingly empty life, I could take up the cause of girls such as the one who'd just gone past. After that I went back to bed and slept.

When I'd breakfasted, I slept again and was still asleep when someone called, "Vinnie — Vinnie. Wake up."

The voice was a familiar one, a girl's, and for a little while I tried to tell myself that I was back in my room at The Bananas but I knew damned well I wasn't.

"Stop foxing, Vinnie." A hand grabbed my foot through the bedclothes and shook it. "Come on, Mum, wake up," the voice said and I opened my eyes.

A bar of sunlight lay across the room and standing in it was Clare. She'd cut her hair. That was the first thing I noticed. I couldn't very well miss the fact because although the back of it was still a fall of pink-shot auburn, the hair around her face was short and jellied into spikes. She'd worked on her eyebrows too, plucking them almost to extinction and I must admit that this piece of vandalism emphasised the beauty of her eyes. Having seen that much, my own eyes gave full marks to the tilt of her cheekbones and the sweetness of pale un-painted lips.

She'd grown taller since we'd last met and inside her clothes, which incidentally would have gladdened the hearts of the kids who lived on the jetty, her seventeen-year-old body was as thin as a boy's.

"Coo-coll," sang the dove outside and I wanted desperately to hug my skinny daughter but all I did was say, "How did you get here?"

Taking care to look past the bridgework on my nose, she said, "Uncle Bart rang me from Rockhampton. Apparently the hospital had been in touch with him."

"Poor Bart."

Clare lifted one shoulder. "I don't think he wanted to be bothered." Her tone was as noncommittal as mine, not that I listened anyway. I was too busy pleasing my eyes with the sight of her.

Growing self-conscious under the stare she looked away and said, "I flew from Melbourne this morning." A pause. "I was planning to visit you anyway."

"Where did you get the money?"

"I had some and borrowed the rest."

After that I couldn't think of anything to say and while I reached for a pillow on the chair next to me then pushed it behind my back, I was thinking, I've got to keep the conversation going because if I grow dumb this time there may never be another chance.

I don't think Clare noticed my silence. She'd moved closer to the bed and suddenly she hoisted her backside onto it and after fishing in the pocket of her pants, produced cigarettes and matches.

Watching her light a cigarette, I wanted to say, "How can you be a dancer if you smoke?" But I didn't let myself.

She knew what I was thinking anyway because after puffing out some smoke she said, "They're only herbal ones. I've given up really, I started again after Uncle Bart rang. I won't buy another packet."

"Then why do it now?"

"You don't understand anything, do you?" said Clare and getting off the bed went to stand at the window with her back to me.

Neither of us spoke. I was looking back down the wretched tunnel of the past and no doubt she was doing the same thing. The silence stretched on until I had no idea how to break it. Then suddenly, Clare leaned out the window and said, "There's a yacht going past. A dark one with smoky brown sails."

"A schooner, is it?"

"With two masts and an orange blaze on the stern."

"Yes, that's the one. 'Damascus' it's called and I'd like

to sail over the edge of the world on it."

"Who owns it?"

"I've no idea but if ever I coveted anything, I covet that."

Clare bobbed back into the room and turned to look at me. There was a child-glow of pleasure on her face but it faded quickly and in a voice a fraction above a whisper, she said, "Why did you let Pandora take me from you?"

With presence of mind that surprised me, I said, "I didn't. I went to Con Smythe and got you back."

"Pandora said public opinion made you do that."

"Pandora would."

Clare was silent, watching my face. Then she moved, came to stand back by the bed and still watching me, said, "Is it true you've got a lesbian lover?"

"Who told you that?"

"The woman next door."

I was picturing Mrs Parsons, her neighbour in Melbourne, a valium addict with a half-bald Pekinese dog, when I heard Clare say, "The woman in the next ward. She said you had this girl friend and were planning to run off with her."

"Faith Bogle! How on earth did you meet her?"

"This morning when I got here, I told the sister outside that I'd come to see my mother. Without asking who I was, she said, 'The second door on the right around the corner.' So I went to that ward without looking in here."

"Of course," I said, "she saw the auburn hair." And I began to laugh. I laughed the way I'd done the night before, but this time I stopped as soon as the wound on my face began to hurt.

My eyes were on Clare's when that happened and as plain as day I saw her feel the pain in her face too. Indeed her hand flew up to touch the spot. It was an extraordinary moment, a mind-stopping one because it showed me the bond which had so delighted me when she was born was still there. Not only that but I was able to look back and recognise the thing I'd seen on her face four years before when she'd crouched against the Chinese tapestry in the hall. And what I recognised was need. Clare had needed my love and was praying that I in turn had the need to give it. No doubt, I told myself, the same expression had been stamped on my face in the days when I held my breath and waited for Irene to show that she loved me as well as Bart.

So all along the arctic zone between Clare and me was of my making not hers. Sliding down a little in the bed I asked myself why I'd seen none of that before. Was my coldness part of my mourning for Brook — some hideous hair-shirt I'd chosen to wear? Was I simply afraid of love because I'd learned what happens when you lose the object of it? Or worse, was I bent on punishing Clare because I saw her as another version of vulnerable Vinnie Seymour?

The answer was beyond me, but it was time I knew to set things right between my daughter and me; time to say a sentence so perfect it would sweep away the past and set us together on some daisy-pied path into the future. I knew though that to find such a sentence I'd need a lifetime and already Clare was waiting for me to speak.

I was still mulling over it all when she said, "*Are* you?"

To gain a minute or two, I said, "What was the question again?"

"You know damn well what it was." In saying that, Clare sounded so like me, my heart lightened in spite of everything and pushing myself up against the pillows again, I said, "Go off with Marcia? Certainly not. You see there's this other girl, a skinny dancer who likes the odd cigarette. She's the one I'd like to sail away with."

As declarations of parental love go, I guess it was a little thin, yet it made a smile show itself at the corners of Clare's mouth and although she said, "Be serious," her voice was soft.

"I am serious."

"Then tell me about the lesbian. Is she really wanted by the police?"

"You and Faith had quite a talk didn't you?"

"Not really. She seemed terribly surprised to see me and rushed into an explanation of how you came to be injured. When it dawned on me that her husband was the one who attacked you, I excused myself and came in here."

Thinking, I'll bet Faith was surprised, I said, "Okay, I'll tell you about Marcia. She's a psychologist turned taxi driver who came to live at The Bananas. The night before last she stole Victor Bogle's vintage Jaguar and shot it off the Toomey lookout into the sea."

"Accidentally?"

"No, she meant to do it."

"For God's sake — why?"

"She was making a feminist statement."

"Is she some sort of crazy?"

"Not at all — a little intense perhaps but I'm sure that if you'd met her, you'd have liked her. I did."

Watching me again, Clare said, "Is it true that you were lovers?"

I tried out one or two flippant replies in my mind but deciding that the moment called for an attempt at honesty, I said, "There was one occasion. It was no big deal and not repeated."

I saw my daughter accept the reply and find it satisfactory. "Where is she now?"

"Somewhere down in New South Wales and still travelling, I'd say."

"What will happen to her?"

"Nothing probably. Marcia's smart enough to find some place as isolated as The Estuary and lie low there until all this blows over."

"And then?"

I gave a puff of laughter. "Then she'll probably make another of her feminist statements and move on again."

"Will you be seeing her?"

"I can't answer that except to say I wouldn't be surprised. I've a feeling she'll turn out to be the kind of comet that zips through one's life at more or less regular intervals."

While Clare was digesting that, I leaned forward and touched her arm. "Come on — it's your turn to talk. You said earlier that you were coming to see me anyway — what about telling me why?"

Instead of answering, she put the packet of cigarettes on the bed and looking down at it, spun it around with her finger.

I was dwelling on the way her lashes made fans of chestnut against her skin when she lifted her eyes and said, "I've met someone too."

The words, God not yet, rushed through my head, then Clare was speaking again. "I needed to talk to someone about him and when I worked it out, I realised the only person I could trust was you."

Filing away the compliment with one or two her father had paid me, I said, "Go on, tell me about it."

She pushed the cigarettes aside and hoisting her bottom onto the bed gave me a smile which I'm certain flew straight up from the heart. "His name's Nick and he's Greek, or rather his parents are. He was doing Law at Monash but dropped out to work for the peace movement."

"His parents would love that."

"Yes, you can imagine. There was a series of earth-shaking rows and now he doesn't see his family any more. He says he doesn't care, but of course he does. Anyway, he thinks I should give up my course too."

"Why, for God's sake?"

"He says it's an indulgence by which he means there's no point in training to be a dancer if there's no one left to dance for."

"And you, Clare, what do you think?"

"I don't agree. I see it the other way. It seems to me there's no point in saving a world that doesn't have room in it for joyous things. So we argue endlessly about it and I try to show Nick that my commitment to the dance is also my commitment to the future — my *belief* in it. And I tell him I'm prepared to work for his cause as long as I'm free to work for mine as well."

I can't tell you how proud I was of my daughter then — not only of her words, though God knows I was proud of them, but there was more because while speaking, she'd jumped off the bed and held her arms before her in the universal gesture of giving. Every part of her, voice, body, even it seemed the air around her was imbued with the quality of fire or poetry or whatever it is that Art demands of its favourites — the quality I'd believed was missing when I saw her dance at the college break-up in Melbourne.

I'm sure Clare guessed how I felt and wishing no doubt to forestall my bravos, she leaned forward, looked closely at my face and said, "Hey, that cut's beginning to heal already."

In spite of the change of subject, I think she was pleased with the way things were going because she spun away from me and did a complicated little dance step which took her as far as the patch of sunlight beyond the end of the bed. There she spun to face me again and with the dancing mood still on her said, "Mum, I was wondering if you'd come back and work for the peace movement too."

It took me a minute to catch my breath and when I did I said, "You mean you want me to work for Nick in order to get you off the hook?"

The pleasure left her face and fixing her eyes on two oxygen cylinders standing on a trolley by the wall, she said, "You could put it that way."

"In that case, I'd better fit it in."

At first she wasn't sure I meant it, then she beamed at me and gave a delighted little shiver. "I was afraid to ask," she said.

"Clare, we've spent the past years being afraid of each *other* and it's time we stopped, but to get back to the business of dancing, while it means anything to you at all, don't give it up for any man because if you do, you'll end up empty-armed and at the mercy of the winds like old Pandora Hunt."

"God forbid," said Clare and because we both needed to let off steam, we laughed immoderately.

Her face rosy with amusement, Clare danced back to me. "Speaking of old friends, this came last week." She pulled a dogeared letter from her pocket and flourished it. "It's from Hannibal. She's pregnant again."

I flopped back against my pillows. "Wow, that's a surprise."

"It was for Hannibal too, because y'see..." Clare paused there to give me a look I couldn't read. "The marriage's bust, finished, *kaput* and she wants to come home."

"Clare, that's terrible."

"Because she wants to come home?"

"Of course not. Because the marriage is in trouble."

Pocketing the letter again, Clare said, "Last year Alan

had a fling with this starlet at Cannes or somewhere. Hannibal thought it was over but it seems the girl followed him to Paris and they've been seeing each other ever since."

"Christ!" I said the word on behalf of my friend Hannibal but found myself repeating it in a whisper as I watched a nurse help a woman in a dressing gown shuffle past the door. The woman, who was tiny and bent with age, had a bow of vivid pink on the end of her stiff little white plait. In the crook of her arm was a golliwog. The little group took a long time to cross the doorway and as it did, the nurse called to me, "Sister says you can leave any time this afternoon."

I was still thinking about the old woman with her ribbon bow and her golliwog when my daughter said, "Hannibal thinks you won't approve of her coming home. That you'll expect her to stay with Alan and make a go of things."

With my daughter back in focus, I said, "Don't be mad. She must do what's right for *her*. Besides . . ."

"Yes?"

"I've missed her every day since she left."

"Good. I'll pass that on." Clare was about to say something else but was stopped by the arrival of Loretta in full uniform. She said she'd come to check on my condition but judging by the way she studied Clare when introduced, I'd say that wasn't the entire truth.

We chatted for a while and when Loretta left, Clare said, "I'll leave too. I want to move your things to Grandma's house."

I grinned. "You may find it hard to get a taxi."

"Someone will help, I'm sure." She plonked a kiss on my undamaged cheek and headed for the door but stopped halfway there to look back at me and say,

214

"Another old friend of yours turned up in Maryston recently."

"Who was that?"

"William Standford Boland. You know... the man you nicknamed Beauregard."

"Clare! I don't believe you."

"It's true — I swear. He went there looking for you, and old Birdie Dadswell sent him down to me."

"Keep going — I'm agog."

"So you should be. He's put on weight if you want to know and become quite fat. The day was a freezing one, about twelve degrees, and Beau was wearing silk but I guess he's too well insulated to feel the cold."

"What did he say, for heaven's sake?"

"Just that he wanted to see you."

"Is he back for good?"

"He said he didn't know but I can tell you one thing — he won't take off again without seeing you. He made that clear." After watching my face for a few moments, my daughter surprised me with a matey sort of wink, then left.

After lunch, I was imagining myself meeting Hannibal at the airport when a kite loomed into that portion of sky framed by my window. It was shaped like an ant with feelers, big bug eyes and a nipped-in waist. From it, floated a long tail of pink and yellow.

Telling myself that only the Chinese had the patience to make such a thing, I got up and went to the window to find out who owned it.

The kite flyer was on the headland by the beach — a clumsy creature with an outsize body and what seemed to be too many arms and legs. As I watched, my dog Billie appeared from nowhere and rushed towards it. When she did, the figure broke to become two people, both female and both holding the string of the kite. They were some distance from me but I had no trouble recognising one as Clare. Moments later I realised the other had the unmanageable hair and slightly knock-kneed stance of Hannibal Ballinger.

"The pair of monkeys. She was here all long," I thought as Hannibal stepped back to let Clare fly the kite alone. At first she was no match for the ant. It swooped and fluttered perilously close to the river but my daughter persevered and in a little while had it sailing serenely in the bare blue sky. When that happened Hannibal turned to look up at my window so I grabbed my big white hospital towel and in the manner of someone surrendering the fort, used both hands to wave it at her. Then, grinning to myself, I went towards the locker where my clothes were.